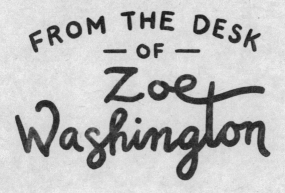

FROM THE DESK
— OF —
Zoe
Washington

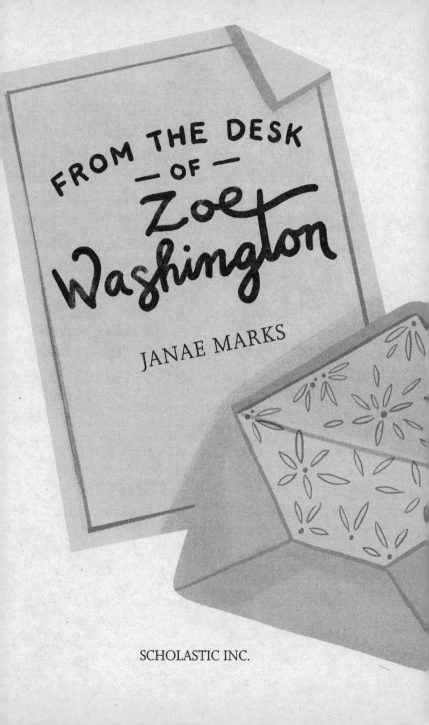

FROM THE DESK
— OF —
Zoe Washington

JANAE MARKS

SCHOLASTIC INC.

ISBN 978-1-338-75914-3

12 11 10 9 8 7 6 5 4 3   21 22 23 24 25 26

Printed in the U.S.A.   40

First Scholastic printing, January 2021

Typography by Laura Mock

For my mom and my daughter,
my biggest inspirations

Chapter One

The day I turned twelve, I was certain it'd be my favorite birthday yet, but then I got the letter.

I'd just had my dream birthday party at Ari's Cakes. Mom's friend Ariana owned the bakery in Beacon Hill, my favorite neighborhood in all of Boston. It had cute brick buildings and town houses, with cobblestone streets. There was a deli with baskets of fresh fruit for sale outside, a chocolate shop, a coffee shop, and a ton of fancy restaurants. And then there was Ari's Cakes, with its pretty, pale-blue awning and a wooden sign above it with the store's name written in white script. Her front window always had lots of cupcakes on display along with fresh flowers. You could smell the sugar before you walked in.

Even though it was pouring rain outside, I felt like the luckiest girl. I'd been in a professional kitchen with my best friends, Jasmine and Maya, as we baked and decorated chocolate fudge cupcakes.

When my parents and I got home, Dad pulled his rain jacket hood onto his head and rushed inside with the box of leftover cupcakes. Mom, using an umbrella, carried my gift bags. I hurried behind them, and on my way in, grabbed the mail from the mailbox next to our front door.

While I kicked off my sneakers in our foyer, I flipped through the envelopes, checking to see if my great-aunt's birthday card arrived. She usually included money, and I was dying to add an egg separator to my baking supplies.

There was a catalog and some junk mail from credit card companies. And then I spotted a plain white envelope with my name, Zoe Washington, and my address handwritten in neat, blue print.

I glanced at the return address and froze. "Massachusetts State Penitentiary" was typed on the upper left corner, across from a waving American flag stamp. The name Marcus Johnson was written in that same blue handwriting above the prison's name.

It was a letter from my convict father, a man I'd never heard from before. I couldn't believe it.

Just like that, my birthday didn't matter anymore.

The envelope slipped from my fingers, landing on the floor. My dog, Butternut, ran over and started licking it, but I snatched it up and dropped it onto the table next to the front door.

Why would Marcus write to me? Why now?

I only owned one picture of him, which Grandma had given me, since Mom would never approve. It was one of Mom's pictures that Grandma had saved from when Mom and Marcus were high school sweethearts. I'd hidden the picture between the pages of one of my journals. In it, Marcus was at a Boston Celtics game, wearing a team sweatshirt and a huge smile. My smile looked like his, which was weird. Someone I never met had the exact same smile as me. And his brown skin matched mine. Mom's skin was a little lighter.

Now Marcus was sitting in a prison cell, probably wearing an orange jumpsuit. That's how I imagined people in prison.

I bet he didn't smile much there.

I picked up the envelope and rubbed my thumb across the seal, but all of a sudden, my fingers stopped working and I froze in place. I wanted to read it, but I was also terrified of what it might say. He'd committed a terrible crime. What if he'd written something scary? It was only a piece of paper, but the feeling wouldn't go away.

I took a deep breath and started to open the envelope again, but then I heard Mom come down the stairs. I knew it was Mom and not my stepdad, Paul, because she was humming a song, which she did a lot, especially in front of the bathroom mirror when she was putting on makeup. She had a pretty good voice, but she always said it was because of the bathroom acoustics. That was wrong, because my stepdad sometimes sang in the shower, and the acoustics didn't stop him from sounding like a dying coyote.

I quickly tucked the letter into the pocket on the inside of my rain jacket. It wouldn't be a good idea to show Mom. I was pretty sure she'd take it away without letting me read it. I hoped she couldn't hear how hard my heart was beating.

"I put the gift bags in your room," she said.

"Thanks."

"Did you have fun today?" she asked. "Your cupcakes came out so pretty."

"It was amazing!" I told Mom.

But now I couldn't focus on how amazing it was, not with Marcus's letter taking up so much space in my brain.

"This today's mail?" Mom stared at the foyer table, where I'd left the rest of it.

"Yup. I grabbed it from the mailbox."

"Thanks." But then her eyebrows scrunched together, and her shoulders did what they did when she was stressed—they lifted up toward her ears. She smiled at me, but it was a forced smile, like she wasn't actually happy. She picked up the pile of mail, and as she flipped through it, her shoulders slowly returned to their normal position.

"I thought Auntie Lillian's card might've come, but I didn't see it." I swallowed hard, thinking of the letter that *had* come. I wondered if I should tell Mom about it. But what if it made her mad or upset? She didn't like to talk about Marcus.

Mom smiled at me for real. "It'll come. Anyway, there's one more birthday surprise for you. We're going to order Hawaiian-ish pizza for dinner."

I forced myself to smile. "Hawaiian-ish" was the name I'd given my favorite pizza combo—pineapple and pepperoni instead of ham. Since my mom and stepdad thought it was gross, we usually only got those toppings on half a pie.

"Sounds great." I cleared my throat. "I'm gonna go to my room, and, um . . . put my gifts away."

It was a total lie, but that's not what Mom noticed. "You're not going to take your jacket off?" she asked.

Marcus's envelope was still in my pocket, right over my heart, which was beating fast.

"I'll take it off in my room." I walked away before Mom could say anything else.

What could Marcus have to say to me?

I had to know.

Chapter Two

I shut my bedroom door and opened the envelope. The paper inside was a piece of loose-leaf, like what Mom would buy to put into my school binders. The words filling the page were written in the same blue handwriting from the front of the envelope, except the print wasn't as neat. I stood in the middle of my bedroom and read the letter from start to finish. And then I read it again. Everything was quiet except for my heartbeat echoing in my eardrums.

To my Little Tomato,

Happy Birthday. I can't believe you're twelve

years old. Wow. Do I sound like a broken record when I say that you're growing up so fast? Do you even know what a broken record is? Everybody used to listen to CDs when I was growing up, but my dad—your grandpa—kept a record player in the corner of the living room. He always says that music sounds better coming from a record player. He might be right. His favorite singer is Stevie Wonder. Have you ever heard any of his songs? He has a pretty great voice. There's this one song called "Isn't She Lovely." You should look it up sometime. Stevie's saying exactly how I feel about you, my baby girl. Well, you're not a baby anymore, but I know you've gotta be pretty lovely at this age.

I wish I could give you a hug and see your smiling face on your big day. I'm sorry I can't be there to celebrate with you. I know your mom is doing something special. She was always good at knowing how to celebrate birthdays when we were together.

Even if you never reply to these letters, I'll keep writing them. Though I hope you'll write

8

*me back one day. In the meantime, I want you
to know that I think about you every day.
　Love,
　Daddy*

All I could do was stand there staring at the paper in my hands. I was like the Tin Man in *The Wizard of Oz* when he needed to be oiled. My arms and legs felt stiff, like they'd weigh a million pounds if I tried to move them.

Why did Marcus sound so . . . nice? Mom always made it seem like he was a bad person. He didn't seem like he was writing from prison. I wasn't sure how someone in prison would sound, exactly, but I guessed they wouldn't be so smart.

He seemed normal. He liked music, like any other dad. Like my stepdad, who was into classical and jazz music. I'd heard of Stevie Wonder, and I thought I knew a couple of his songs. I'd look up "Isn't She Lovely" later.

I read the letter again. Why had he called me Little Tomato? It was kind of weird. I liked tomatoes, especially the little ones, but I didn't want to be *called* one.

What did Marcus mean when he wrote "these letters"? This was the first one I'd ever gotten from him. It didn't make any sense.

None of this did.

I stared at my striped rug as a million thoughts swirled around my head like cake batter in a mixer.

Should I write him back? What will happen if I do?

I had no idea Marcus thought about me. But what if he was pretending to be nice to me because he wanted something from me? What, though?

Maybe I should throw the letter away.

There was a knock on my bedroom door, which made me jump two feet and almost drop the letter. I clutched the loose-leaf paper in my now-sweating hands.

"Hey, Zoe?" It was Mom.

I tensed up. "One second!" I stuffed the letter back into the envelope and tucked it underneath my purple comforter. I remembered I was still wearing my jacket, so I took it off and threw it over the back of my desk chair.

Then I cracked my bedroom door open.

"Trevor's here," Mom said.

Trevor? What's he doing here?

As if she could hear my thoughts, Mom said, "He wants to give you his birthday present, since he wasn't at your party."

There was a reason for that: he wasn't invited.

"Can you tell him I'm busy?" I whispered.

Mom's glare made it clear she was not about to do that.

"Please? It's my birthday, and . . . he's not my friend anymore." *Not after he made our friendship out to be a total joke.*

Mom's expression softened a little. "When are you going to tell me what happened?"

I shook my head. No way was I telling her anything. She'd probably force me to forgive Trevor, and that was not going to happen.

"You know, as a brand-new twelve-year-old," Mom said, "you're old enough to understand how rude it'll be if you don't come out and thank him for the gift in person." She forced my door open wider. "C'mon."

All I wanted to do was read Marcus's letter again and figure out what it all meant, and what I should do next.

But first I had to deal with my ex–best friend.

Chapter Three

I trudged behind Mom to the living room, where Dad was talking with Trevor's mom, Patricia.

Trevor usually celebrated my birthday with me. We were in the same grade and had been neighbors practically our whole lives. Our families shared a two-family home—a baby-blue house with two side-by-side white front doors, a wooden porch, a paved driveway, and a two-car garage.

During the summer, my friends Jasmine and Maya always left town. Maya would go to sleepaway camp in the Catskills, and then on vacation with her parents and younger sister. This year they were going to San

Francisco. As for Jasmine, she normally spent the whole summer at her grandparents' house in Maryland with her twin brother and cousins. But this summer, she was actually moving to Maryland. Her parents decided they wanted to live closer to her grandparents all year round. When I said goodbye to Jasmine at the end of my birthday party, I cried, having no idea when I'd get to see her next.

I'd stay home for the summer, as usual. Mom didn't believe in spending thousands of dollars for summer activities when I could have fun at home for free. Like always, Grandma would watch me while my parents were at work.

I never really minded being home for the summer, because I'd always had Trevor. We'd come up with our own adventures, like riding our bikes around our neighborhood or making s'mores using the microwave. Last summer we watched all the Marvel movies on Trevor's dad's big-screen TV. Sometimes, Trevor would help me bake cookies or brownies. We never got bored when we were with each other.

But this was not going to be like all our other summers. A month earlier, Trevor betrayed me and I hadn't talked to him since. I had no idea how I'd entertain myself without him, since bike riding and movie marathoning didn't sound as fun alone. I couldn't even complain to

Mom because she'd tell me to use my imagination, or say that being bored was good for me.

When I walked into the living room, Trevor was standing next to the couch. I narrowed my eyes at his baggy Medford Middle School Basketball T-shirt. He probably wore it over here on purpose, to rub it in my face that he only cared about the team. He was playing that old-school Mario game on his phone again. I recognized the beeps and cheery music coming from the speaker. But then he lowered his phone and his eyes locked with mine. I looked away.

The thing was, I knew Trevor way too well. Even though I only saw his face for a second, I knew what that look meant: (a) he didn't want to be there either, and (b) he was still confused about why I was mad at him. Well, I wasn't about to tell him. He should be able to figure it out for himself.

"Happy birthday, Zoe!" Patricia came over and gave me a hug. "Your dad said you guys were at a bakery. Sounds like you had a good time."

I thanked her while thinking, *Why would he do that?* I didn't want to have to explain why Trevor wasn't invited along. But lucky for me, Patricia didn't say anything about that.

"Trish, do you want a cupcake?" Mom asked her. "We have a lot left over."

What? Those were my cupcakes. I crossed my arms.

"It's the best chocolate cupcake I've ever had," Dad added. "And I'm not just saying that because Zoe made them." He winked at me.

I glanced over at Trevor, who was standing up straight now, peering toward the kitchen. He couldn't resist anything with chocolate.

Back when we still hung out together, Trevor and I spent a lot of time making and eating snacks, especially chocolate ones. One time he was so desperate, he sucked the coating off chocolate-covered raisins, even though he hated raisins.

"Just eat the whole thing," I'd told him before popping a chocolate-covered raisin into my mouth. "They're good."

"They're shriveled-up grapes. Like mini grape corpses. Disgusting." He'd sucked the chocolate off another one and then reached the spit-covered raisin out to me. "Since you like raisins so much, you can have mine."

"Eww!" I'd grimaced.

He'd pushed it closer to my face, so I'd stood up to get away from him. Then he'd chased me around my house with it. We made several laps around the kitchen island and ended up in the living room, where we collapsed on the couch, laughing so hard that tears streamed from my eyes.

My throat tightened. It was hard to imagine laughing like that with Trevor again.

"Girl, I can never say no to cake," Patricia was saying with a laugh.

Mom laughed too. "I'll get you a couple."

Patricia followed my parents down the hall, leaving Trevor and me behind.

I wished I could leave Trevor alone and go back to Marcus's letter, but I'd get in trouble if I did that. Instead, I leaned against the doorway between the living room and hallway, ready to make my escape as soon as I could.

Trevor and I were quiet for a few seconds, and then he said, "Happy birthday, by the way."

It didn't sound like he really meant it, which made me want to kick him in his shins. "Why are you even here?" I asked. To apologize for what he said about me? To make it up to me on my birthday?

"To give you your present," he said.

"I thought you'd be hanging out with one of your *teammates*." I said the word "teammates" as if it tasted like burnt cookies and sour milk.

Trevor shrugged.

I huffed and turned away. Fortunately, that's when my parents and Patricia returned from the kitchen. Patricia held a Tupperware filled with two cupcakes.

"I hope you like your present, Zoe." Patricia pointed to the wrapped rectangle on the coffee table. "We should get going. I have the night shift." She was a nurse at Massachusetts General Hospital and was already wearing her pale-blue scrubs. Her pressed hair was in a neat bun on top of her head.

Mom gave me a look that meant, *What do you say?*

Right. "Thank you," I said, looking only at Patricia.

She smiled and said goodbye, and Trevor followed her out without another word.

I was about to head back to my room when Dad said, "Let's see what Trevor got you."

I didn't care what Trevor got me. But Mom and Dad were staring at me, waiting for me to open the gift, so I sat down on the couch and unwrapped it.

It was a cookbook. But not any cookbook. The new one by Ruby Willow, the thirteen-year-old pastry chef I was obsessed with. She'd won a kid baking competition on the Food Network. My dream.

I grinned as I flipped through the pages, which had pictures to go along with the recipes. S'more brownies. Fried Oreos. Peanut butter and jelly macarons. Yum!

"Isn't she that chef you like?" Mom asked.

"You told them to get this, right?" I asked her.

Mom shook her head. "Actually, your dad and I were

going to get it for you, but then Trish called and asked if it'd be a good gift idea. She said Trevor suggested it."

"Oh," I said. It was probably before I stopped talking to him. Whatever. I wouldn't let that stop me from enjoying the cookbook. "I'm going to my room now."

I was done thinking about Trevor. Marcus's letter was way more important.

Chapter Four

I sat on the porch steps with my earbuds in while Butternut napped in a patch of sun at my feet. It was the best kind of summer morning—not too hot, not too sunny, and not too many mosquitoes out to bite me. Our dead-end street was quiet. The only person I could see around was our older neighbor across the street, who was watering the hydrangea bushes lining his front yard with a hose.

I was listening to Stevie Wonder's "Isn't She Lovely," which I'd downloaded the night before. I had heard it before, though I wasn't sure when. Maybe Mom had played it at some point, or it was in the background of a movie. How weird that it reminded Marcus of me. We were complete strangers.

If Marcus was such a monster, why would he like listening to Stevie Wonder? Stevie's music was so upbeat and happy. It didn't add up. Maybe Marcus was lying to me. It was hard to tell.

I decided to write him back, just this once. Maybe I could get some answers—why he did what he did. Whether he cared at all that I was going to be born. Was he writing to me now because he felt guilty?

On my lap was a journal Jasmine got me for my birthday, which had a Z made of flowers on the cover, and a purple pen. Tucked into the back of the journal was Marcus's letter, which I'd read a hundred more times. I decided to write a draft of a letter back to Marcus in the journal. Getting the words out could help me figure out how I felt and what I really wanted to know from him.

Before I could start, I heard the creak of a storm door opening and closing behind me. It woke Butternut up, and he ran to the top step to see who was coming outside. I didn't have to turn around to know it wasn't my door that had opened—it was Trevor's. His was the only door that creaked like that. Trevor's parents had left earlier, so either Trevor or his older brother, Simon, had come outside.

I glanced back. Just my luck: it was Trevor. If it was last summer, I would've been excited to hear him come out. It'd mean the start of one of our adventures.

But not anymore. I hoped he was on his way out so he wouldn't hang around. He was probably going to spend all summer with the basketball guys.

Butternut ran over to Trevor, and his collar jingled as he jumped up Trevor's leg, asking to be pet. Butternut didn't care that Trevor and I were in a fight. I wished he would give Trevor the cold shoulder, too.

Instead of leaving, Trevor sat down on the other side of the steps and took a book out of his cargo shorts pocket— *The Golden Compass*. From his other pocket, he took out a red sports drink and a small bottle of sunblock, which his mom always insisted he wear during the summer.

Butternut flopped back into a sunny patch on the steps between the two of us.

I tried to ignore Trevor and go back to my journal. But I could see him out of the corner of my eye. He was acting like everything was normal, like this was a regular Sunday with us hanging out together on the porch, playing go fish or spit. Right then, he was squirting big globs of sunblock onto his hands and rubbing it into his brown skin until the white lotion disappeared. The scent—a mix of chemicals and coconut—filled the air.

"Do you have to be out here right now?" I took my earbuds out for a second and put my journal down on the step.

Trevor looked up from his book. "It's my porch, too. I'm on my side."

Trevor's family lived in the left side of the house. He was currently sitting on the left side of the wooden porch steps. As if to make his point, he scooted even closer to the left railing until he touched it.

I didn't have a good argument, so I scooted even farther to the right of the porch steps. I put my earbuds back in and raised the volume a little more, letting Stevie Wonder's singing voice fill my ears.

I picked up my pen and started to write.

Dear

What should I call Marcus? I couldn't call him Dad. Paul had been my dad ever since Mom married him when I was five. He might look nothing like me, with his olive skin and hazel eyes, but he was my dad in all the ways that mattered.

I sometimes called adults by their first names—like Trevor's mom, Patricia. But that was because I'd known

22

Patricia forever, and at one point she told me to call her that.

I crossed out "Dear" and started over.

~~Dear~~
Hi,

Even with that settled, I had no idea what to write next.

I got your letter, I began. I was really surprised since I never thought I'd hear from you. I—

There was a tap on my shoulder, so I looked up. Trevor. He had scooted down toward my end of the porch steps. Now he was clearly in my space, with Butternut happily wagging his tail next to him.

Trevor's mouth was moving, and when he realized I couldn't hear him, he pointed to my earbuds.

I yanked them out. "What do you want?"

"What're you writing?" he asked.

"Are you kidding me?" I stood up.

"What?" Trevor rubbed one of his eyes.

"I'm not talking to you."

"Why not?"

"Because!" I said.

"That's not a reason," Trevor said.

Butternut barked and jumped up my leg.

I sighed loudly. I couldn't even write a letter on my own steps without Trevor messing it up. "Forget it. Take the whole porch if you want. I'm going inside." I turned toward my door with my journal tucked under my arm.

"Hold up," Trevor said.

I took a deep breath and got ready to yell at him to get a clue already, but when I faced him, he was holding Marcus's letter. Which must've fallen out of my journal. It was unfolded, and he was reading it.

"What are you doing? Stop it!" I snatched the letter from him. "That's mine. It's private."

Trevor put his hands up in the air, but looked me straight in the eyes. "Is that from your dad?"

I stopped short. "What are you talking about?" I tried to keep my face even and make my voice sound casual.

"Your dad that's in jail." Trevor paused, and then said, "He's there because he killed somebody, right?"

My breath caught in my throat. "How do you know that?"

Even though Trevor and I used to be close, I never told him about what Marcus did. I didn't want to talk about it with anyone. Trevor, Jasmine, and Maya knew my birth dad was in prison, but not why.

I hated that this person related to me was a monster. A murderer. It made me want to throw up. He could be

24

locked up for the rest of his life, but there was a chance he could get out early after serving twenty-five years. It was called "parole." I sort of hoped that wouldn't happen.

Trevor shrugged. "Your mom told my mom once. They were in our kitchen, and I was coming down the hall. They didn't know I could hear them."

"When?" I asked.

Trevor thought about it. "Last year or something."

"You never told me."

"I didn't know if you knew. It seemed like a secret or something."

"Oh." I wasn't sure what else to say.

Trevor stepped closer to me. "Why aren't you talking to me? And why didn't you invite me to your birthday?"

There was a long pause before I said, "I know what you said about me."

His eyebrows scrunched up. "Huh?"

I didn't want to repeat the words. Plus, I was in the middle of something, and Trevor was getting in the way. Again. "I don't have time for this right now," I told him.

Before Trevor could say anything else, I turned around and began to storm inside. But then I remembered something important and turned back.

"One other thing. You better not tell anyone about the letter. Seriously, you cannot tell *anyone*. If you do, I . . ." I paused. "I'll never, ever forgive you."

"I won't tell," Trevor said, his face serious. "Even though you won't say why you're mad at me. You can't ignore me forever."

Watch me.

Before Trevor could say anything else, I went inside, Butternut trailing behind me.

A moment later, I heard Trevor's storm door creak open and closed. With my journal and Marcus's letter in hand, I ran down the hall to my room. Now I could focus on what really mattered.

Chapter Five

Almost an hour later, I finished the letter.

June 26
Hi,

    I got your letter. I was really surprised since I never thought I'd hear from you.

    I'm not sure what to call you. I can't call you Dad because Mom's husband, Paul, is my dad. Mom taught me to always call adults by Ms. or Mr. whatever their last name is, unless they say it's okay to use their first name. Am I allowed to call you Marcus? This is all kind of weird.

I listened to the Stevie Wonder song "Isn't She Lovely." It's nice. I started listening to some of his other songs too. I really like "Signed, Sealed, Delivered (I'm Yours)." We don't have a record player, but I do know what one is. I downloaded some of his songs to my phone.

Part of me wants to know more about you, but I don't know what to ask you, what to ask someone in prison. What I really want to know is why you did what you did.

I was happy with it so far—except for that last line. I wanted to know why Marcus committed his crime, but I was scared to ask. Scared of the answer. He didn't seem like a bad person in his letter, but that didn't mean he wasn't one.

I decided to cross that line out. Maybe if I sent another letter, I'd ask him then, when I felt ready for whatever answer he had to give.

Part of me wants to know more about you, but I don't know what to ask you, what to ask someone in prison. ~~What I really want to know is why you did what you did.~~

Also, why did you call me Little Tomato?
Sincerely,
Zoe

In my desk drawer, there was a box of stationery that my grandmother had given me for my eleventh birthday. I didn't usually send letters to people, so I'd never used it before. But now it was exactly what I needed. I took out a sheet of the stationery—it was fancy white paper with one dark purple line going around the perimeter. On the top in script were the words:

From the Desk of Zoe Washington

The pretty paper made me feel more grown-up, like I knew what I was doing.

With my journal open beside me, I rewrote my letter on the stationery in my neatest print. This was really happening.

When I was done, I wrote Marcus's prison address on the envelope. I wondered how far away it was, so I did a quick search on my computer. Less than an hour drive, but I hadn't been to that part of Massachusetts before. I sealed the letter and went to grab a stamp from the junk drawer in the kitchen.

The next morning, I waited for my parents to leave for work, then got ready to head to the blue mailbox at the corner of our street. I didn't want to leave Marcus's letter in the mailbox at our house and risk my parents seeing it. But before I could step onto the porch, I heard familiar voices: Trevor and his basketball friends, Lincoln and Sean. I went to the living room and glanced out the window. They were standing at the bottom of the porch steps, talking and laughing about something. Trevor dribbled a basketball while Lincoln and Sean held on to their bikes. They weren't even wearing helmets!

My hands balled into fists.

Please leave. I waited for Trevor to get his bike and ride away with them. But they didn't leave. Instead they all went to the driveway to play basketball.

What do I do? I could go outside through the back door, but I was pretty sure they'd still see me. After what happened, after what they'd said about me, I didn't want to face those boys.

Would I be stuck inside my house all summer, forced to listen to their voices and laughter echoing throughout my own house?

I went back to my room to wait. I cleaned it up a little and unpacked my school backpack. I smiled when

I pulled out the notebook I shared with Jasmine and Maya. It was one of those black-and-white marble composition notebooks, but we'd covered the front and back with pictures and quotes we'd found online. My favorites were the quote that said, "Dance like nobody's watching," and this adorable picture of otters holding hands. We used the notebook to write notes to each other. After each of us wrote a note, we'd pass it to the next person, who'd pass it to the third person, and we'd do that over and over all year long. Passing notes wasn't allowed in class, but nobody realized we were writing notes when we wrote them in a regular notebook.

I flipped through and read a few pages, laughing at our inside jokes and missing those girls even more. Maybe I could start a new summer notebook, and we could mail it around to each other—like *The Sisterhood of the Traveling Pants*, but different. But Maya probably couldn't mail something so big from camp. And Jasmine was gone for good now. Next year, I wouldn't be able to write notes to her at all. Would Maya and I even make another notebook without her?

Forget it.

Instead, I sent a message to our group text, knowing Maya wouldn't see it until she was done with camp, and Jasmine's grandma made Jasmine keep her phone off most of the time.

Me: Just unpacked our notebook from this year. I miss you guys already!!!

My heart hurt. Who knew if we'd even text as a group anymore once school started up again.

I put the notebook in my desk drawer with the others, and then spun around in my chair a few times until I got dizzy. Then my eyes landed on the Ruby Willow cookbook sitting on my nightstand. I got up and lay across my bed, leaning on my pillow with the cookbook in front of me.

Ruby was on the cover wearing a white chef's coat and hat, with her blond hair in her signature side braid. She had the biggest smile, and held up a plate with three fruit tarts on it. The strawberries, blueberries, and raspberries looked so fresh, the vibrant colors popped off the page. I wished I could reach into the picture to taste them.

I flipped to Ruby's bio in the back of the book, even though I already knew everything about her baking career—how she used to bake all the time with her mom, and then became a contestant on the Food Network's *Kids Bake Challenge!* She hadn't been a front-runner the whole time. A boy named Frankie won a few of the earlier challenges, so everyone expected him to win the whole competition. Not me. I didn't like him very much.

Even during the challenge that the kids complained about the most—where they had to make a six-layer rainbow cake—he kept bragging about how he'd made rainbow cakes a million times at home, and it would be a "piece of cake." He thought he was *so* funny.

Mom and I watched the show together, and we never stopped rooting for Ruby. She didn't pretend to know everything, and she worked really hard at every challenge. She also liked helping other people. There was one time she finished a cookie challenge early, and another baker, Tessa, was running behind. Tessa had taken her sugar cookies out of the oven when there were only five minutes left and still had to decorate them. Ruby helped her out by piping on some of the icing. Tessa didn't get sent home that episode, and it was all because Ruby helped her.

There was one challenge where Ruby had to make pie, and she ended up in the bottom two. She'd gotten flustered while baking, so her pie crust design looked messy. Plus, they also had to make ice cream and hers didn't turn out so well. I was literally at the edge of my seat watching that episode. But then this other girl Lindsey went home instead, because her pie crust was still raw. Ruby looked so relieved and shocked. She ended up winning the next challenge and made it to the finale against Frankie. Everyone was surprised that she won, but I knew she had it in her all along.

Looking through the cookbook made me want to watch Ruby's season again, so I grabbed my laptop. I opened up the *Kids Bake Challenge!* website and was about to click on the Full Episodes button when a banner on the side of the page caught my attention.

IS YOUR CHILD A PASTRY CHEF IN THE MAKING?

Are they between the ages of 12 and 14?

Food Network is looking for the best young bakers in the country!

Click here to apply by September 15.

I was twelve now. I could audition for the show myself!

I clicked on the button, which brought me to the application. Mom or Dad would have to fill it out for me. Mom knew how good of a baker I was and even told me I could be the first Black girl to win the show one day. I'd told her I wanted to compete when we watched it together, and she said we could talk about it when I was old enough.

I spun around in my desk chair again, but this time it was a happy, excited spin.

I'd seen every single episode more than once, so I knew how the competition worked. I could spend the summer practicing baking to get ready, which would give me something to do without Trevor.

If I won, I'd be just like Ruby Willow! It would be a dream come true. I never saw many Black pastry chefs on the shows I watched, or in the cookbook section of the library, but I was still determined to be one when I grew up.

I read through the application and rules for applying as I imagined myself on the cover of my own cookbook. Then I turned on an episode of the show, peeking out of the window every once in a while to see if Trevor and his friends were still outside.

In the middle of watching my second episode of *Kids Bake Challenge!*, I finally heard the boys go inside Trevor's house. I paused the episode so I could sprint to the mailbox.

I was covered in sweat when I was done, but at least my letter to Marcus was on its way.

Chapter Six

If I was going to keep Marcus's letters a secret from Mom and Dad, I had to make sure I checked our mail before they did. This wasn't hard during the week when they were at work and I was home with Grandma. I paid special attention to our mail delivery for three days, and figured out that our mail carrier always came to our house between twelve and twelve thirty p.m. I set an alarm on my phone for noon so I could look through the mail as soon as it arrived.

On Saturdays I would have to make sure I got to the mail before my parents did. On the first Saturday after I mailed my letter to Marcus, my parents and I went to breakfast at the Broken Egg. It was a hole-in-the-wall place in Davis Square whose menu had twenty different egg dishes and another twenty pancake varieties. We always got there early, before it filled up with college students. The three of us squished into a tiny wooden booth in the corner of the restaurant. When our food arrived, it took up the whole table. Dad got eggs Benedict with a side of potatoes, and Mom got a veggie omelet with fresh avocado on top. I got the triple-berry pancakes, which were sprinkled with powdered sugar. They were the fluffiest pancakes ever, and I loved that they were both sweet and tangy—my favorite combination.

"I want to ask you something," I told my parents between bites.

"The answer's yes," Dad said.

How did he know what I was going to ask?

But then he said, "You *do* have powdered sugar on your nose," and smiled.

"Dad! That wasn't my question!" I laughed. Still, I wiped my nose off with my napkin. "Okay, so, you know Ruby Willow, the girl who wrote the cookbook Trevor gave me, is twelve like me," I said. "Well, actually, I think she's thirteen now, but she was twelve when she won the baking show."

Mom picked up the creamer and poured some into her coffee mug, which had the restaurant's logo: an illustration of a cracked egg with a smiley face. "Of course. She won the *Kids Bake Challenge!*"

"Yes! That's her."

"That's the show where that one kid made a brownie look like a hamburger, right?" Dad asked. He didn't usually watch the show with us.

"Right!" The episodes where the contestants had to make "dessert impostors"—desserts that looked like savory foods—were always my favorites.

"So Ruby Willow won. And she got twenty. Thousand. Dollars." I said it slowly, for effect.

Dad almost choked on his orange juice. "Did you say twenty thousand dollars?"

I smiled. "Yup. The winner also gets to publish their own cookbook. Like Ruby Willow's."

"Wow. Well, that is impressive."

"I know. She's amazing. Remember how I said I wanted to be on the show? Well, I just found out that the Food Network is about to cast the next season, so you can apply until the middle of September. I'm finally old enough. Will you fill out the application for me?"

Mom and Dad gave each other a look, like they weren't sure how to answer.

"It would be an amazing learning experience," I added. "I've been baking at home for so long, but if I got on the show, I could learn from the mentors and judges—real, professional bakers."

"You're sure you want to be on TV?" Dad asked.

"I want to win the competition, and it's on TV, so yeah . . ." To be honest, I was a little nervous about the being-on-TV part, but I was pretty sure I could handle it. It wasn't like I would be acting in a sitcom or something. I'd just be myself.

"I know I said we could talk about this when you were old enough, but I'm not sure . . . ," Mom said.

"Why not?" I asked. "If I won, the money could go into my college fund."

"True," Dad said. "When does the filming happen? During school?"

"I'm not sure," I said.

"And I assume you have to travel somewhere for the filming?" Mom asked. "I didn't think they filmed in Boston."

"I don't know . . . ," I said.

"Hmm," Mom said, giving Dad another meaningful look.

"Before you say no, let me get you more of the details," I said. "You always say you can't make an informed decision until you know all the facts, right?"

"That's true," Mom said.

"Great. I'll show you the website when we get home," I said. It would be the perfect distraction while I snuck off to check the mail. "In the meantime, it's not a no, right?"

"It's not a no," Dad said.

"But it's not a yes either," Mom added.

It was a maybe. I could work with that.

The next morning, Mom and I headed to the farmers market, which we did most weekends during the summer. We'd get to the market right when it opened at nine a.m., so we could see the best selection. We'd learned our lesson two summers earlier when we got to the market later in the morning and all of the best produce was gone. Sometimes there was live music. Today, a girl was playing a pop song I recognized from the radio on her violin.

"Are Jasmine and Maya gone yet?" Mom asked me as we walked along the different tables, keeping our eyes out for free samples.

"Yeah. I miss them."

We stopped in front of a fruit vendor. On the table were little blue cardboard cartons of blueberries, blackberries, and raspberries, and the tarts on the cover of Ruby Willow's cookbook sprang into my mind. Then I remembered the recipe for lemon blueberry pie that was inside it, so I picked up a container of the blueberries.

"Can I get these?" I asked Mom.

"Sure. Let's get some of these cherries, too." She grabbed a carton of those and walked to the guy behind the cashbox to pay. "I know you hate when they go away, but you still manage to have fun during the summer, right?"

I did, back when I still had Trevor.

"I guess," I said.

I grabbed one of the blueberries before Mom put the carton in her tote bag and popped it into my mouth. It was perfectly juicy.

Mom turned to me and pushed her sunglasses to the top of her head. "Okay, so I have some good news."

"What?" I asked.

"Your dad and I looked at the website for the cooking show you want to be on."

I gripped Mom's arm. "And?"

"And . . . we're not sure you're ready for something like that."

I let go of her and frowned. "I'm ready!"

"Just listen. We're not sure right now, but we're going to give you a chance to prove it to us."

"Do you want me to bake all of the recipes in Ruby Willow's cookbook? Because I can." I'd already thought that it would be good practice. "That's what the blueberries are for."

We were still standing right next to the fruit vendor, which was getting more crowded by the second, so Mom and I moved out of the way. We ended up in front of a table with different homemade soaps and lotions that smelled like vanilla and lavender. Some of the soaps had pressed flowers.

"That sounds great," Mom told me as she smelled one of the soaps. "But what do you think about doing an internship at a bakery this summer?"

"What do you mean?" I asked.

"I talked to Ariana last night, and she said she can always use extra help during the summer, since the bakery is extra busy. You can go over and help her out once a week, and she can also teach you some of her baking tricks."

"Are you serious?"

"Yup. If you do a good job—if Ari gives you a positive review—then at the end of the summer, you can apply to the Food Network show."

I couldn't believe it. I could be on the *Kids Bake Challenge!* and intern at a real, professional bakery.

"Thank you so much!" I tackled Mom with a hug.

She laughed as she hugged me back. "You're welcome. But don't get too excited yet. You still have a lot of work to do. Working in a bakery is not easy."

I could totally handle it.

"When do I start?"

"Tomorrow. Dad will drop you off on the way to work, and you'll stay for the first half of the day. Then he'll pick you up around lunchtime. How does that sound?"

"Amazing!" I grinned.

If I was gone for only half a day, then I could still check the mail for a letter from Marcus when I got home.

I hated that I had to pay so much attention to the mail. But maybe I wouldn't have to.

We continued our loop around the market and passed by four vendors before I built up the nerve to say, "Mom? Can I ask you something?"

"Of course," she said.

"Would you ever let me speak to Marcus?" I asked. "Like, maybe send him a letter in prison?"

Mom stopped walking and her expression got serious. "Marcus?" She said his name like it tasted rotten. "Why would you want to do that?"

"Because he's my dad. I mean, you know. My birth dad."

"He may have had something to do with your birth, but that's it." Mom's voice hardened. "He's never even seen you."

"Because I'm not allowed to visit him. Right?" I asked.

"Right," she said. "I'm not taking you to a prison."

"But shouldn't I get to decide if I want to know him?" I asked.

"When you're an adult, if that's what you want, I can't stop you. But right now, you're still a child," Mom said.

I frowned. "You act like I'm a baby. I'm twelve now, practically a teenager."

Mom shook her head. "There's still so much you don't know."

"So tell me!"

I didn't mean for it to come out so loud. A few people turned their heads to look at us.

Mom pulled me away from the center of the market, and we ended up next to a big oak tree. She put her hands on my shoulders and looked me in the eyes. "Listen to me. Marcus is not a good man. He lies and manipulates people. And he's a convicted murderer. I don't want him in your life. You have to understand." She paused. "Where is this coming from? Why are you asking about this now?"

"No reason," I mumbled.

"Are you sure?" Mom asked.

"Yes."

"Okay, then. I don't want to talk about this anymore." She exhaled. "Let's go home."

I silently followed Mom to where we parked our car. My chest felt tight.

Mom wasn't being fair. I wasn't a little kid anymore. I was old enough to figure out for myself how I felt about him. Besides, Marcus couldn't hurt me from behind bars.

I had no choice—his letters would have to stay secret.

Chapter Seven

Dad and I got "the look" again on our way to my first day at Ari's Cakes. The look we got sometimes when we were out together, just the two of us. Dad parked the car a block away from the bakery. As we were getting out, an older white lady walked by and stared at us a little too long, her face twisting into a confused and judgmental glare. I knew exactly what that look meant. She was wondering why a Black girl was getting out of a white man's car. What we were doing together.

My face got hot.

"Hey, Dad?" I said, extra loud so the woman would hear.

"Yes, kiddo?"

"Do you have quarters for the meter?" I asked.

"Yup, right here," he said.

I peered behind me to see if the woman was still staring. But she had gone back to walking.

I shook my head at her. *Good riddance.*

When Dad and I walked into Ari's Cakes a few minutes later, I could see why Ariana had said she needed extra help. The place was packed, with a line weaving around the front area of the shop.

"Do you think it's always like this in the morning?" I asked Dad as we squeezed around customers to get to the counter.

"Maybe it's because everyone's off for the Fourth of July," he said.

"Um, there's a *line*," someone said, and when I turned toward the voice, I saw it belonged to a teenage girl with glasses. She glared at me.

I said, "Oh, I'm not . . . I'm actually . . ."

"Zoe!" I whipped around toward Ariana's voice. She waved me over to where she stood behind the counter in a pale-blue apron—the shop's signature color. She was also wearing a pale-blue baseball cap with the Ari's Cakes logo on it, her wavy brown hair tied back into a low bun. "So glad you're here. It's super busy today."

47

I glanced back at the girl with the glasses, so I could show her that I wasn't cutting the line, that I knew the owner. But now she was staring at her phone. Oh well.

When Dad and I reached the counter, Ariana pulled us behind it and gave me a hug. "Nice to see you, lady. Hey, Paul," she said to Dad.

He was holding up his travel mug. "Mind if I grab some coffee before I go?"

"Sure thing." Ariana took the mug from Dad and filled it. "On the house."

Once he had his mug back, Dad said, "Thank you. Zo, I'll see you at noon. Have fun." Since it was a holiday, he didn't have to go to work, so he'd be the one to pick me up when I was done.

After I said goodbye, Ariana brought me to the back. It was less hectic than the front, but not by much. There were fewer people back there, but they were all bustling around, getting work done. The kitchen smelled amazing—like cake batter and chocolate. I'd bottle it up if I could.

"This is our busiest day of the summer," Ariana told me. "Everyone wants cupcakes for their Independence Day barbecues."

"Makes sense," I said.

"I'll introduce you around and give you a quick tour, and then I'll set you up with a project."

A project. I couldn't wait to see what Ariana had planned for me to do. Would I get to help decorate cupcakes? Or use all of their huge equipment to mix batter? Or maybe Ariana would use my help at the front, since it was so busy. I could take the cupcakes out of the case and box them up to hand to the customers. That could be fun, but I really hoped I'd get to help with baking.

Ariana went into a closet and pulled out another pale-blue apron that matched hers, with the Ari's Cakes logo embroidered on it. She also handed me a hat. "Here you go. Now you're an official employee."

The apron was a little big, but I adjusted the neck strap and tied the belt in a bow. I got to wear an apron when I had my birthday party at the bakery, but that one had been plain black. Now, I felt like a real pastry chef. I looked down at it and beamed. I thought about asking Ariana to take my picture, but I didn't want to seem like an amateur.

When I was here for my birthday, I only got a quick look at the bakery's kitchen. We spent the rest of the time in the party room, which had its own professional ovens. This main kitchen wasn't super big, but it seemed well organized. On one side was a wall of ovens, a commercial stove with six burners, and a large sink. On the opposite wall was the biggest stand mixer I'd ever seen in my life.

It was practically as tall as me! I bet I could fit inside the mixing bowl. Next to it was a table with large containers of flour and sugar underneath. Against the middle wall were a few tall cooling racks, and in the center of the room were two long stainless-steel tables.

On one of the tables were several pans of dark-red cupcakes; they had to be red velvet. An employee—a pale girl also wearing an Ari's Cakes baseball cap, with a shooting-star tattoo on her forearm—held a huge piping bag of white frosting, which she piped on the rows of cupcakes faster than I'd ever seen before.

"That's Liz," Ariana said. "She graduated from culinary school a couple of years ago. She's our second-best icing froster. The best being me, of course." She winked.

Liz looked up briefly to give a quick wave and smile before going back to piping.

"Next to her is Corey," Ariana said. Corey was tall and skinny, with dark-brown skin. He followed behind Liz, carefully sprinkling red and blue star sprinkles on top of the cupcakes she'd just iced. "He goes to Boston University. This is his second summer with us."

Corey said, "Nice to meet you."

"Same here," I said.

"This is Zoe," Ariana told them. "She's helping us out on Monday mornings."

I could stare at the Liz and Corey assembly line for hours. It was so mesmerizing to see plain cupcakes become beautifully decorated within seconds. But I couldn't keep watching them because Ariana was already moving on to the next thing. I followed her to the stand mixer. An older man wearing a white chef's coat and a black-and-white bandanna on his head stood in front of it, peering inside as the huge beater spun around to mix the batter.

"Hey, Vincent—this is Zoe. She's our new helper on Mondays." She turned to me. "Vincent is our head pastry chef. He takes care of most of the baking, along with Rosa." She pointed halfway down the room to a woman dragging a huge bag of flour across the floor.

"Hello," Vincent said, barely making eye contact with me.

"Where are we on red velvet?" Ariana asked him.

"Next batch is out of the oven in about five minutes," he told her. "And I'm mixing more batter right now."

"Great." Ariana turned to me. "Our signature Fourth of July cupcake is red velvet with cream cheese frosting. You saw Liz and Corey decorating them. We're selling a ton this morning. Want to try one?"

A cupcake for breakfast? "Yeah!"

Ariana handed me one of the cupcakes Liz and Corey just finished decorating. I took a bite and broke out in a grin. It was delicious. The cake was rich and moist, and the cream cheese icing was so smooth. I gobbled it all up in a few more bites.

With a laugh, Ariana said, "So I guess you didn't like it?"

"It was amazing," I said, reaching for the bottle of water in my backpack.

"Okay, back to work." She led me to a walk-in closet in the corner of the kitchen. Inside were a bunch of shelves holding cardboard boxes. Ariana grabbed a large one and led me back into the kitchen to an empty table. Then she went back and got a few more.

I imagined all the things that could be inside the boxes. Baking supplies? Candy decorations? A secret ingredient?

Ariana opened the first box, and inside was . . . more cardboard. Flat pieces of cardboard in the bakery's signature blue. Ariana pulled some of it out.

"You saw how busy it is out there," she said, nodding toward the front of the bakery. "We're going to run out of boxes pretty soon, so I could use your help putting some more together. It's easy." Ariana showed me how to fold the sides up and tuck them into flaps, so the cardboard transformed into a small box that could fit two cupcakes. "We also have boxes for four, six, and a dozen cupcakes. Think you can do this?"

That was it? I was going to help put together *boxes*?

"Are you sure you don't need help with mixing red velvet batter, or decorating the cupcakes?" I asked. "I can help Corey with those sprinkles. I'm really good at sprinkles."

Ariana saw the expression on my face. "I know this isn't what you expected to do on your first day, but I could really use your help here," she said.

"But—" I started.

"Ariana!"

We both looked toward the voice coming from the other side of the room. It was one of the employees from the front. "Phone call for you."

"I have to grab that." As she started walking away, she added, "Go ahead and get started on these boxes. I'll check on you in a bit."

I sighed and looked at the pile of pale-blue cardboard on the table. Was this all I'd get to do all summer? Make boxes and stare at everyone else while they actually baked? At least I got to see what it was like back there, in a real bakery kitchen. But I'd seen that on TV. I wanted to use the mixer and ovens myself. I wanted to learn how to pipe the icing on the cupcakes like Liz.

But Mom said I could audition for *Kids Bake Challenge!* if Ariana gave me a good review. I had to get to work on

53

the boxes. It was so easy, I probably lost brain cells while doing it.

Pick up a box.

Fold up the sides.

Tuck in the flaps.

Repeat.

While I worked, my mind wandered and I started thinking about Marcus. He had to have gotten my letter by now. What did he think when he read it?

Would he write back? Did I really want him to?

I thought of everything Mom had said about Marcus.

Was I really about to become pen pals with a murderer?

Panic shot through me like icing out of Liz's piping bag. Maybe it was a mistake to write Marcus back.

It was too late to get my letter back now. *Focus on the boxes*, I told myself.

Across the room, Ariana stood next to Vincent, talking to him about something as he scooped batter into large cupcake trays. I could do that. I was really good at scooping batter.

Ariana spotted me and the huge pile of folded blue boxes on the table and gave me a thumbs-up. I made myself smile.

Chapter Eight

If I couldn't bake at Ari's Cakes, at least I could do it at home. On Thursday, Grandma and I were in the kitchen getting ready to make fried Oreos, one of the recipes from Ruby Willow's cookbook. I'd just mixed the batter that we'd dip the Oreos in, and now I was putting some confectioner's sugar into a shaker. We'd shake the powdered sugar on top of the fried Oreos at the end, and eat them while they were still warm and gooey, with mugs of cold milk. Meanwhile, Grandma was busy pouring oil into a pot that was heating up on the stove. She was wearing my mom's red apron over her white T-shirt and jeans.

My apron, which my parents gave me for Christmas, had pastel macarons all over it.

My phone was connected to Bluetooth speakers on the kitchen table. I'd opened the music app and shuffled all of my songs. I was twisting the top back onto the shaker right as a Stevie Wonder song came on—"Superstition." I had downloaded it after reading Marcus's first letter.

"You like Stevie Wonder?" Grandma started bopping her head as she finished pouring the oil, making her turquoise beaded earrings jiggle. She loved fun earrings.

"I heard this song at Jasmine's house once," I lied. "Her dad was playing it. I liked it, so I added some of his songs to my playlist."

"You've got soul. I love it." Grandma wiggled her body as she sang along with the chorus. I started dancing, too.

Then my phone chimed, interrupting the song. It was my alarm set for noon. I practically jumped to turn off the alarm, before Stevie Wonder's voice filled the kitchen again.

"What was that for?" Grandma asked.

"Nothing." I wiped my hands off on a towel and grabbed my phone. "I'll be right back. Don't start without me!"

I bolted down the hall to the foyer and peeked out at our street from the storm door. A minute later, like

56

clockwork, the mail carrier walked up the porch steps. He saw me standing there and gave a quick wave. I opened the door and he handed the mail to me.

"Thanks!" I said.

"Enjoy your day," he said and turned to go.

I let the door close behind me and quickly flipped through the stack. There it was at the bottom, with the same prison return address, the same flag stamp, and my name and address handwritten again. But this time, Marcus had written with black ink instead of blue. The envelope was a little thicker, like there was more than one sheet of paper inside.

My heart raced. I left the rest of the mail on the foyer table and went straight to my room to read it.

To my Little Tomato,

I can't tell you how happy I was to get your letter. I actually shed a few tears and people here thought someone must've died. I can count the number of times I've cried as an adult on one hand. Getting your letter was one of them. Want to know another time? When I first found out your mother was pregnant with you. When she told me, I burst into tears and actually fell down to my knees. I always wanted

57

to be a father, since my dad was always such a great one to me. I wish I'd had the chance to be a better dad to you. When I found out I was going to prison, well, that was another time I cried. I hate that I'm missing out on your life, and so many other things.

But, back to happy stuff. You asked about Little Tomato. It's from a song. You can probably tell I'm really into music. The song is called "Hang On Little Tomato," and it's by a group called Pink Martini. I liked the sound of Little Tomato for a nickname, so I started calling you that. Now you're Zoe, but you'll always be my Little Tomato.

Speaking of names, yes—you can call me Marcus. I understand how weird this is for you. Don't feel bad about that. It's got to be especially strange since it sounds like you never got my other letters. I've sent you a lot over the years, but when I never heard back, I figured either you didn't want to write me, or maybe your mom wouldn't let you. I wouldn't blame her if she didn't. But I kept sending letters so you'd always know that I wanted to hear from you. I'm so glad you wrote back now.

I'm happy you want to get to know me. You can ask me whatever you want, and I promise to answer honestly. You're probably wondering about my life. Prison is not a great place to be, but I try to keep my head down and focus on my studies. I first got here right after I started college. Getting a degree was always really important to me, and I didn't want being in here to change that. It took me a while, but I eventually got my bachelor's degree from a college that mails the coursework to inmates at my prison. I decided to study sociology—why people are the way they are. Now, I'm working on my master's. It helps me pass the time and keeps my brain working. I hope you understand how important it is to have an education. Do you like school? What else are you into?

I hope you'll write me another letter.

Love,

Marcus

My mouth dropped open as I finished reading.

I read the letter again. Was he pretending to be nice, to care about me? He seemed so sincere, so *real*.

My gym class teacher once had us do this relaxation

exercise where we had to lie on the floor, tense up all of our muscles one at a time, and then relax each muscle one at a time. I thought it was pointless, and the mats we were lying on smelled like a hundred sweaty armpits. But by the end of the exercise, I actually did feel better. Looser. Reading that letter, it was like I'd been tensing my whole body for all of my twelve years, and now I could finally relax. At least a little bit.

"Zoe, what's wrong?"

I startled at the sound of Grandma's voice. She was now standing in my bedroom doorway. I gripped the pages in my hand, almost crushing them.

"You were gone for a while." She took a couple of steps closer to me, worry lines all over her face. I sat on top of the letter so she couldn't see what it said.

"What's going on, baby girl?" Grandma asked. "You can talk to me."

I said the first thing that popped into my head. "It's, uh, Maya. She wrote me a letter from camp." The words tumbled out. "I miss her."

Grandma nodded. "I can understand that. I promise she'll be back home before you know it."

I nodded, barely able to look her in the eyes. I couldn't tell her who the letter was really from. She might tell Mom and Dad.

Grandma glanced at my desk and saw the open box of stationery. Her face lit up. "You're using the stationery I gave you."

"Yup." I had to think of a lie—fast. "I'm, um, gonna write Maya back at camp."

"Great." She flashed me a warm smile. "Well, the oil's hot and ready. I don't know about you, but my mouth is watering thinking about these fried Oreos." She winked.

I glanced down at the letter and then back at Grandma. Writing back to Marcus could wait. "Mine too. I'll be right there. Just give me a minute."

"Okay," Grandma said.

She left, and I folded up the letter carefully, putting it back into its envelope. I opened my desk drawer, took out my sixth-grade math notebook, and hid the envelope between two random pages.

That night after dinner, I went into my room, closed the door, and read Marcus's letter again. I knew I'd only planned to write him back one time, but I still had so many questions for him.

I couldn't believe he'd sent other letters, and I'd never gotten them. I wondered how many he'd sent, and what could've happened to them. Maybe they got lost in the mail, or he didn't have my address correct until now. I wish I knew what they'd said.

I grabbed a fresh piece of stationery and put on my headphones. I'd downloaded "Hang On Little Tomato" to listen to as I wrote. It was totally different from the Stevie Wonder song. The first half was instrumental, with only a horn playing the melody, and then a woman started singing along in the second half. She had a really pretty voice, and she sang about hanging on when you felt sad or alone. If you hung on, everything would be all right. I wasn't completely sure what you were supposed to hang on to, but I liked the message—the idea that things would get better eventually. Maybe it meant things between me and Trevor could get better.

It wasn't until the song repeated for the third time that I realized the words "little tomato" weren't even in the lyrics. Why name the song that, then? I thought about it, and figured that Little Tomato must be who the song was for—the person the singer was singing to. The picture on the song's cover was a guy holding a small child in the air. Maybe it was a message to that little kid that everything would be okay. It made me smile.

I thought that Dad would like the song, since it had a jazzy feel to it. I couldn't tell him about it, though. I wouldn't want to have to lie about how I discovered it.

Plus, I kind of wanted to keep the song to myself.

I played it again and started to write.

From the Desk of Zoe Washington

July 7

Dear Marcus,

I'm listening to "Hang On Little Tomato" right now, as I write this. It's not the kind of song I normally listen to, but I like it. I never thought I'd want to be called a vegetable . . . or is a tomato a fruit? That always confuses me. If it's a fruit, then why is it always in regular salads with other vegetables, but never in fruit salad? Anyway, after listening to the song, I don't mind the nickname.

That's cool that you're getting your degree. I like school, too. I know it's not for a long time yet, but I'm excited for college. I really want to go to the CIA. No, not the government CIA. (People always ask me that.) The Culinary Institute of America. My dream is to become a pastry chef and make desserts all day long. This summer, I have an internship at a bakery in Beacon Hill. If I do a good job, my mom will let me audition for a kid baking show on the Food Network. I really want

63

to get on the show so I can win the prize money, and have my very own published cookbook. It'd be a dream come true.

Besides baking, I like riding my bike, reading, and hanging out with my friends. Except right now, I'm sort of in a fight with one of my friends. That's a whole other story. My favorite subject in school is French class. I like languages. I want to become fluent in more than one. Maybe I can even become a pastry chef in France.

What did you like to do when you were my age? Also, I'm curious about your family. Where are your parents? Do you have any siblings?

Sincerely,

Zoe

Chapter Nine

The next morning, after my parents left for work, I poked my head into the living room, where Grandma was reading a book on the couch.

"Hi, Grandma," I said. "Can I walk to the mailbox? I'll be right back. I have a letter for Maya."

Grandma put her book down and then twisted around to peer out of the window. "Isn't it raining outside?"

Streaks of rain slid down the outside of our window.

"I think the mail carrier will take the letter if you leave it in your own mailbox," Grandma said.

"Ours usually forgets," I said, not knowing whether or not that was true. "Anyway, I don't mind the rain. I have a rain jacket, and I'll carry an umbrella. I'm only going to the corner of our street."

Grandma stood up and joined me in the foyer. "I guess that's all right. Hurry back though, in case it starts to thunder."

"Okay." I was holding Marcus's letter, and I tucked it under my chin, address side down, while I put on my rain jacket. As I slipped my left arm into the sleeve, the letter fell to the floor.

Address side up.

Marcus's name was right there in plain sight.

Grandma bent over to help me pick the envelope up, and it was like I was watching her in slow motion.

"I've got it!" I yelped. I bent over and snatched the letter off the floor before Grandma could, bumping heads with her in the process.

"Sorry!" I said as she stood up again, rubbing her head.

"That's okay, baby."

I hugged the letter to my chest as Grandma looked at me funny.

Had she seen Marcus's name and address on the envelope? I couldn't tell from the expression on her face.

Before Grandma could say anything, I grabbed the umbrella from the holder in the closet and opened the front door.

"Be right back!" I said and hurried outside to the mailbox, my heart thundering in my chest.

Trevor was in the back seat of Dad's car when it was time to leave for Ari's Cakes on Monday morning.

I opened the front passenger door. "What are you doing in here?"

Trevor shrugged. "I'm coming."

"What?" I turned to Dad in the driver's seat. "What's he talking about?"

"He's coming with you to your internship," Dad explained. "Just for today. Patricia got called into work, and asked if he could spend the morning with us."

"What about Simon?" Watching Trevor was supposed to be his brother's responsibility.

"He's still in Maine," Trevor said. "Camping with his friends. He comes back today."

"It's only for a few hours," Dad said. "I already asked Ariana, and she said it was fine."

Why didn't anyone ask if it was okay with me? This was so typical.

"Get in, Zoe," Dad said. "We're going to be late."

I jumped into the car and put my seat belt on. Dad pulled out of the driveway and I leaned my head against the window. Not even Dad's light jazz radio station could calm me.

"How's your summer been?" Dad asked Trevor.

"Okay, I guess," Trevor said. "I've been playing basket-ball a lot."

"You're a point guard, right?" Dad asked.

"Yeah."

I stared out the window and tuned them out.

My headphones were in my backpack, so I dug them out and put them on. I listened to music for the rest of the ride.

Dad dropped us off in front of Ari's Cakes twenty minutes later, and Trevor and I got out of the car without speaking a word to each other. But I wasn't going to let him ruin my mood.

It was much less crowded in the bakery than on the Fourth of July. There were only a few customers in line, and Ariana was behind the counter, helping one of them with their order.

"Hey, Zoe. Hey, Trevor," she said when she spotted us.

"Hi," we both responded in unison. I glared at Trevor, wishing he would disappear.

"Zoe, why don't you go grab your apron," Ariana said. "Get one for Trevor, too. I'll meet you in the kitchen."

I headed to the kitchen and stopped at the closet with the aprons. I grabbed one for each of us.

I shoved an apron at Trevor. "Here." In a low voice, I said, "This internship is really important to me. My parents said I can audition for *Kids Bake Challenge!* if I do well."

"Wow, so you might get to be on TV?"

"Maybe," I said.

"That's cool."

"Anyway," I said, "you better not embarrass me here."

Trevor looked offended. "Why would I do that? I didn't ask to come here."

"Why didn't you go hang out with Lincoln or Sean instead?" I asked as I pulled my apron over my head.

Trevor did the same. "Too last minute, I guess."

I glared at him again.

"When are you going to tell me why you're mad at me?" Trevor asked.

There was no way I was going to talk to him about that here. But before I could answer, Ariana appeared. "So, Zoe, remember Vincent, our head baker?"

I nodded.

"You're going to shadow him today while he bakes a few batches of cupcakes."

I smiled. "Cool!" Finally, I'd get to do some baking.

"He's expecting you. Don't forget to wash your hands."

Trevor walked to the sink behind me. While we washed our hands at the sink, I scanned the room and spotted Liz mixing blue food coloring into a bowl of icing and Corey rolling out some red fondant—this thick, Play-Doh-like icing. Rosa was taking a tray of cupcakes out of the oven.

Trevor followed me to Vincent at the huge stand mixer. That morning, he was wearing a dark-purple bandanna.

"Hi," I said. "Ariana said I'm—I mean, we're—helping you today."

"Right," he said. "I have to make five hundred mini cupcakes for a charity event."

"Wow. What charity?" I asked.

Vincent shrugged. "Don't remember the name. That's Ari's job. I just bake what I'm told. Something to do with education, I think."

"Interesting," I said, imagining possible cupcake decorations. They could make little fondant pencils, and maybe even some fondant apples, with little worms poking out. That would be so cute. Maybe that was what Corey was making with the red fondant. Hopefully I'd get to help with that part.

"Better get started," Vincent said. I watched closely as he turned the mixer on. First he put butter and sugar into the large metal bowl. When they were all mixed together, he slowly added a bowl of eggs he'd already cracked. I kept waiting for Vincent to stop and let me try a step—like adding in the flour and milk, which he did next—but he never did. I'd thought he might share a baking tip, but he didn't say a word. It was like he'd forgotten I was there.

"This is boring," Trevor said to me in a low voice. "Why isn't he letting us do anything?"

"Shh." I kept my eyes on Vincent as he added more flour and milk to the batter.

"I thought the whole point of an internship is so that you can learn how to do this stuff, too."

"Would you be quiet?"

"Hey, Mr. Vincent?" Trevor asked, but not loud enough for Vincent to actually hear.

"What are you doing?" I hissed at Trevor.

"I'm gonna ask him if you can help."

"You don't have to do that," I said.

"You do it, then," Trevor said. "Aren't you getting bored just watching?"

I wasn't bored, but I *did* wish I was doing something more. I thought this internship would be more hands-on. So far, all I'd gotten to touch in this place was cardboard.

"Okay. I'll ask him," I whispered.

"Excuse me? Sir?" I tried to speak loudly enough to be heard over the mixer.

Vincent glanced up at the two of us as he turned the mixer off. "Yes?"

"I was wondering if I could help with the next step?"

71

I glanced at the table next to the mixer, which had a few large mini cupcake pans. There was also an ice cream scoop next to them. "You're going to scoop the batter next, right? I can help with that."

Vincent looked hesitant. "I don't think so. This order is very important, and we can't afford to start over because a kid messed something up."

I'm not a kid. I'm an intern. "I won't mess it up, I promise," I said. "Let me scoop a couple and show you."

Vincent still looked unsure. Then Ariana came over.

"How's it going over here?" she asked.

"Great," Trevor said, smiling. "Vincent said he's going to let Zoe scoop the batter."

I stared at Trevor.

"Actually, I'm not really—" Vincent started.

"Sounds good," Ariana said. "Zoe, you only want to fill each cup in the pan about halfway, so there's room for the batter to expand." She picked up the ice cream scoop. "Want to give it a try?"

I beamed and grabbed the scoop from her. Vincent had to get out of my way in order for me to reach inside the mixing bowl. He didn't look too happy about it, but I ignored him as I scooped up some batter and then dropped it into the pan. It was so easy; I didn't know how anyone could mess it up.

"Perfect," Ariana said. She went over to Vincent and put her hand on his shoulder, whispering something to him that I couldn't hear.

I scooped the rest of the batter into the pans, and then Vincent lifted them into the oven. He clicked a timer on it.

"Right. This oven will warn us when it's almost time to take the cupcakes out, at the eighteen-minute mark. While we wait, we can start the next flavor," Vincent said, taking the dirty bowl out of the mixer.

While he did that, Trevor whispered to me, "You're welcome."

I scowled at him. "For what?"

"You got to scoop the batter because of me." He looked satisfied with himself.

"Because you lied to Ariana."

"It was a tiny lie," Trevor said. "You got what you wanted, didn't you?"

"Yeah, but . . . I told you not to mess this up for me."

"I'm not. I just made it better for you."

Vincent cleared his throat, and I looked up at him. The mixer now had a shiny new bowl in it. "Are you ready to bake," he asked, "or do you need more time to finish your argument?"

My face suddenly felt as hot as the oven. "I'm ready."

I glared at Trevor one more time, and then set out to ignore him for the rest of the morning.

Chapter Ten

Trevor and I didn't say anything to each other for the rest of our time at Ari's Cakes, and after Grandma picked us up, we stayed quiet during the entire car ride home. When Grandma pulled in front of our house, Trevor's brother's car was parked in the driveway, with the trunk still open. A rolled-up sleeping bag and duffel bag were on the ground. Simon, a taller version of Trevor but with glasses, came out of the house and picked up the sleeping bag, tucking it under his arm. He waved when he saw us.

"Thanks for the ride," Trevor said to Grandma before jumping out of the car.

Grandma looked at me, her hands still on the steering wheel. "You okay?"

"Fine." I unclicked my seat belt and reached for the door handle.

"Wait," Grandma said, putting her hand on my leg. "You want to run an errand with me?"

I glanced out the window at Trevor helping Simon bring more camping stuff inside. "Yes, please," I said, and put my seat belt back on.

When I realized Grandma was driving to Cambridge, I knew exactly where she was taking us: her favorite tea shop, Cambridge Tea Room. They sold loose teas in all sorts of interesting flavors. Some of them even tasted like baked goods, like blueberry muffins and banana nut bread. There were always multiple Cambridge Tea Room containers on the counter in Grandma's kitchen, and she even left one at our house.

When we got there, Grandma went to the counter to place her order while I went to see what samples they were giving out that day. According to the cards on the two dispensers, that day's sample flavors were a cold watermelon mint and a warm chocolate chai. I filled two small cups with each. The chocolate chai was yummy and smelled amazing. I didn't love the watermelon one, so I poured myself another sample of the chocolate tea to get rid of the taste.

Then I joined Grandma at the counter. "What flavors are you getting?" I asked.

"Another container of green ginger, my favorite. And I'm going to try the new pink lemonade flavor. It sounds summery."

"It's really good," the lady behind the counter said. "I love your earrings, by the way."

Grandma's earrings of the day were blue, yellow, and black-and-white feathers hanging down from gold studs.

"Thank you," Grandma said, beaming.

Grandma got pink lemonade tea for both of us, plus chicken salad sandwiches with salt-and-pepper chips. Then we sat down at a table near the window.

"I want to talk to you about something," Grandma said when we were done eating.

"Okay. About what?" I took a sip from my cup. Even though it was hot, the tea tasted refreshing, like pink lemonade would.

"Your father. Marcus."

I coughed, and tea dribbled down my chin. I wiped it off with my napkin.

"You saw his name on my letter," I said, tensing up in my seat.

She folded her hands on the table. "Yes."

I tried to read Grandma's face, but I couldn't figure out what she was thinking.

"Mom and Dad don't know about it," I admitted.

"I figured that," Grandma said.

"How?"

"If your mom knew, she would've told me."

"Am I in trouble?" I braced myself for another lecture about why I shouldn't communicate with Marcus.

"Not at all." She sipped her tea.

"I'm not?"

Grandma sighed. "It's natural to want to know about your father."

"Even if he's a criminal?" I asked.

"Even if he's a criminal," Grandma repeated.

The worry deep down in my belly lifted up and away like the steam from my teacup.

"How long have you been writing to Marcus?" she asked.

I wasn't sure if I should tell her, but it seemed like if anyone would understand, it might be Grandma.

"Not long," I said. "He sent two letters, and I sent two back."

Grandma nodded. "That time I saw you with a letter in your room? It wasn't from your friend at camp, was it?"

I shook my head.

"You were upset. Are the letters bothering you?" Grandma asked.

"No! In that letter, Marcus said that he wanted me, before I was born. I wasn't expecting that." A lump appeared in my throat.

"I see," Grandma said.

"Do you think Marcus is bad?" I asked. "He sounds nice when he writes to me, but he's in prison for doing something terrible."

Grandma shook her head. "You know, there are multiple sides to everyone. People aren't so black-and-white. Sometimes good people do bad things, and bad people do good things."

"So, you think Marcus is only somewhat bad?" I asked.

She opened her mouth as if to say something, but then changed her mind and closed it.

"What?" I asked.

"I think Marcus is a good person at heart," she said.

"I kind of want to keep writing to him," I told Grandma. "I still have so many questions. But Mom can't know about this." I paused. "Will you keep my secret?"

Grandma exhaled. "I don't know, baby. I shouldn't keep secrets about you from your mom."

"Please? I promise I'll tell her. I just want to write a few more letters to Marcus. Before she makes me stop. You know she won't let me write to him."

A few long seconds passed as Grandma stared thoughtfully out of the window.

"You're probably right," she said, looking at me again. "I still don't like the idea of lying to my daughter, but this situation is not normal. And I think your mom has been stubborn. She's let her own feelings about Marcus get in the way."

Grandma paused, and then said, "How about you give him my address instead. You can read his letters at my house. But I'll read each of them first, to make sure they're okay."

"Really?" I asked.

"Yes. But you have to come clean with your mom," Grandma said. "Before the summer is over."

"Okay." I had no idea how I would tell my mom about this, but I'd figure that out later. "I guess I'll write to Marcus tonight and give him your address."

"Good idea. I'll mail it for you tomorrow."

I leaned over and gave Grandma a hug. She smelled like the lemonade tea and honey. "Thank you."

"Of course." She squeezed me back. "I love you, baby girl, you know that?"

"I love you, too."

From the Desk of Zoe Washington

July 11

Dear Marcus,

I told my grandma about these letters, and she's glad I'm writing to you. Do you mind sending your letters to her house instead? Her address is below.

I paused and pressed the back of the pen against my chin. I thought about what Grandma said about people not being black-and-white. Maybe that's how Marcus was—he did something terrible, the worst thing I could imagine. But at the same time, he'd been sweet to me in his letters and had interesting things to say. I still wanted to know more about him. Maybe he'd changed and was a better person now.

The one thing I'd been holding back talking to Marcus about was his crime. Before I could change my mind, I started writing again.

81

I've been wondering about what you did. I know a little about it. I don't want to think about you being a murderer, not when you've been so nice to me in these letters. Are you sorry you did it?

Zoe

PS Please send another song. I started making a playlist called "Little Tomato's Playlist." I thought you'd like that.

Chapter Eleven

On Saturday morning, I walked into the kitchen, itching to bake something. I opened the fridge and spotted Mom's container of raspberries. She liked to put them with granola on her yogurt for breakfast. The container was still almost full, so I took it out, thinking of the raspberry crumb bar recipe in Ruby Willow's cookbook. I was pretty sure we had the rest of the ingredients I'd need. I ran to get the cookbook from my room.

Mom was in the kitchen refilling her coffee mug when I got back.

She watched as I found the recipe and started pulling flour, sugar, and butter from the cabinet and fridge.

"Can I use the oven?" I asked, since that was the rule. "And can I use the rest of your raspberries?"

"Yes, and yes," Mom said. "Would you like some help?"

"That's okay," I said as I grabbed the rest of the ingredients and organized them in the order I needed to use them. I was old enough to bake by myself, just like I was old enough to write to Marcus. Not that Mom understood that.

"Are you sure? I'd like to help."

I silently put on my apron.

"C'mon, it'll be fun. I'll be your . . . what's it called? Side chef?"

"Sous-chef," I corrected as I turned the oven to preheat. "But I don't need your help." I got out the mixer and some utensils.

"Okay," Mom said, sounding a little disappointed. She sat at the kitchen table with her coffee.

If Trevor and I were still friends, he could help me bake. He'd probably ask me to sneak some chocolate into the recipe. Actually, white chocolate would taste pretty good with the raspberries. Maybe I should make a white chocolate drizzle to go on top.

No. *What's the point? Trevor isn't going to eat them.* My heart sank a few inches.

I started on the raspberry preserves, rinsing off the berries and dropping them into a small pot on the stove with some water. Once it was simmering, I partially covered the pot and got to work on the crumble.

I cracked an egg into a mixing bowl and then measured two and a half cups of flour.

"Are you still mad at Trevor?" Mom suddenly asked, as if she could tell I was just thinking about him. "You haven't been hanging out with him."

I groaned.

"Have you talked to him about it?"

"No."

"You should."

I stared at the mixing bowl as the ingredients transformed into a crumbly mixture.

"I know he misses you," Mom said.

Did he miss me? It seemed like he was doing just fine without me.

"You get it from me, you know," Mom said. "I have a hard time letting things go, too. But think of it this way. You're the one holding all this pain inside of you, which hurts you more than it hurts Trevor. If you can forgive him, it might help you let go of the pain. And you'll get your friend back. It's a win-win."

Then Mom added, "That doesn't mean you have to forget what he did. There's a difference."

Why was she lecturing me? "Can you please butt out of it?" I said. "I really don't need your advice."

"Okay," Mom said quietly. She stood up from the table and grabbed her coffee. "I'll leave you to it."

As she left, I thought of Marcus. It didn't seem like Mom had forgiven him—for what he did, for not being there when I was born. That was why she didn't want me to talk to him. But then again, what he'd done was way worse than what Trevor did to me.

Maybe I'd talk to him.

All of a sudden, I smelled something funny. The preserves! I ran to the stove and pulled the lid off the pot. The raspberries inside were all burned. Either I hadn't put in enough water or I left the heat on too high.

Great. I turned the stove off and put the pot of burnt raspberries into the sink. There were no more raspberries left, and I didn't feel like asking Mom to get me more. I took the bowl off the mixer and dumped the insides into the trash. Then I took off my apron and threw it on the floor.

Later that week, Grandma gave me a letter from Marcus. As my parents were leaving for work, she slipped the envelope to me. I went straight to my room to read it.

To my Little Tomato,

I got your last two letters. Actually, I started responding to the first one when the next one arrived.

I remember your grandmother well. She was always nice to me back when your mom and I were dating. Her house was always like a second home to me. Does she still drink a lot of tea? She used to always love her tea.

As to your question about my crime. I promised you that I would answer all of your questions honestly. I can't give you much from in here, but I can give you my word—I will never lie to you.

I hoped you wouldn't ask about this, because it opens up a can of worms. There's no easy way to put this: I didn't do it. I'm innocent. I have an alibi and there was even a witness, but I'm in here because my lawyer couldn't prove that I didn't do it. Even after we appealed my conviction. It's unfair, but nothing can be done.

I'm sorry that I'm in here instead of out there with you. I'm sorry that you've had to deal with a father in prison. If I could go back and somehow fix it, I would.

I want to end this letter on a happier note. You asked what else I like to do. When I was your age, besides basketball, I played a lot of video games. I was also into drawing. I would draw the characters from my favorite games and cartoons. I used to think I was pretty good, but I stopped in high school when basketball started taking up all of my free time.

You know what else? I liked to cook! I used to help my mom all the time with her recipes, which were passed down to her from her mom. Even now, I get to cook some. My job here in prison is working in the kitchen. My favorite part is chopping the vegetables. I get in the zone and it's pretty relaxing. I never baked much, but it's great that you love baking. When you get on that show and win, I want a signed copy of your cookbook, okay? I hope one day I get to taste one of your recipes.

As for my family, I do have one sibling—a brother who's five years older than me. He lives in Atlanta with his wife and two daughters, and my parents moved down there to be closer to them. Unfortunately, my relationship with them isn't the same now that I'm in prison. I really hope that changes someday.

Here's another song for your playlist. I like all kinds of music, but my favorite has to be R&B. It reminds me of when I was growing up. Look up "Water Runs Dry," by Boyz II Men. That song brings back some good memories.

Please give your grandmother a big hug for me. And tell her to give you one for me too. :)

Love,
Marcus

Chapter Twelve

I sat on the edge of my bed and clutched Marcus's letter between my fingers.

He said he was innocent. Just thinking the words made me dizzy. He couldn't possibly be innocent if he'd been in prison my whole life. Mom would've told me if he was. That meant she must've been right about Marcus all along. He was a liar.

If he was lying about this, he was probably lying about everything else, and I'd fallen for it. How could I let myself believe a convict I'd never met?

I scanned the letter again to make sure I hadn't read it wrong. His *a*'s looked a lot like mine. I hadn't noticed that before. But the words were the same—Marcus really said he was innocent.

A mix of disappointment and anger shot through me. I crumpled up the letter and threw it in the trash, spinning away from it in my desk chair.

But what if Mom or Dad found it when they took the garbage out? I took the letter out again and stuffed it into the bottom of my backpack instead.

It wasn't raining when Dad and I left for Ari's Cakes on Monday morning, but by the time he dropped me off, it was pouring. Sheets of water rolled down the cobblestone streets of Beacon Hill, and the sidewalks were filled with people holding umbrellas.

Dad frowned as he twisted around to check his back seat. "I don't see an umbrella. I'm sorry. You want to run in?"

"Yeah, okay," I said. "Bye, Dad."

"Bye, kiddo."

I jumped out of the car and sprinted to the shop. It was only a quarter of a block, but by the time I walked inside, my T-shirt had big water drops all over it, and my right sock and sneaker were drenched from accidentally stepping into a big puddle.

I stopped at the bathroom to wring the water out of

my sock, and then grabbed my apron from the closet in the kitchen.

"Morning, Zoe." Ariana waved me over. "Come see what we're working on."

I joined her at the metal table in the middle of the room. Vincent, Rosa, Liz, and Corey were also standing around the table, staring at six cupcake pans that looked like they'd just come out of the oven. The cupcakes were similar in color to gingerbread and had a similar spicy smell. None of them were frosted. Each pan had a small strip of blue tape on its edge with different writing in Sharpie. The pan right in front of me said "20 minutes, 1/2c fig," and the one next to it said "18 minutes, 1c fig."

"So, Zoe," Ariana said. "Vincent and I have been working on a new flavor for the shop, using a new ingredient for us—figs. These are fig-spiced cupcakes. If we like how they turned out, we'll roll them out this fall."

"Cool!" I imagined what fig-spiced cupcakes might taste like. Tangy and sweet at the same time. "That sounds really yummy."

"Hopefully they taste yummy, too," Ariana said. "We baked six batches. We wanted to test out three different baking times to see which one gives us the best cupcake texture. And we also baked different amount of fig pieces into the batches, so we can see which ones taste the best."

"Did you use a recipe?" I asked.

Vincent scoffed. "The only recipes I use are in here." He pointed to his head, which was covered with a blue bandanna.

Ariana said, "We modified our spice cake recipe. That's why we have to taste all of these cupcakes to see if the new flavor works."

I nodded. I had no idea this was how pastry chefs came up with new flavors, but I liked the sound of it.

Vincent pressed down on a couple of cupcakes with the back of his finger. "I think they're cool enough now."

"Great." Ariana pointed to the first pan. "We baked these for eighteen minutes, and used more fig pieces. Dig in."

I grabbed a cupcake and took a bite. The cake itself was really good, very moist, but there was maybe too much fig. I looked around the table and everyone looked like they were chewing very seriously.

"Too much fig," Corey said.

Liz nodded. "And the cake's a little underbaked."

Vincent just frowned.

"I agree," Ariana said. "Let's try the ones with less fig that we baked for twenty minutes."

We each grabbed one of those. One bite and I could tell it was way better than the first one. I finished the whole thing.

"It's very good," Rosa said. "Right texture. Right amount of fig."

"I'm diggin' this one," Corey said.

Vincent stayed quiet as he chewed, but he nodded like he was impressed with himself.

"I agree," Ariana said, smiling. "Let's try the others, to make sure this is our winner."

While everyone grabbed the next cupcake, I ran to my backpack, which I'd left inside the supply closet with the aprons, to get my bottle of water. When I reached inside the bag, it felt wet from the rain. I dumped everything from my backpack onto the floor. It wasn't a lot—my wallet, phone, journal, lip balm . . . and Marcus's letter. It was still a crumpled ball of loose-leaf paper, now with a water stain. I stared at it for a second, and the word "innocent" popped into my head.

What if Marcus *was* telling me the truth? He said he wouldn't lie to me. Did innocent people end up in prison?

No. That was ridiculous. Marcus had to be lying. I had to forget about him and his letters.

I stuffed the crumpled ball back in the bottom of my bag. Then I wiped everything else dry on my apron and closed my backpack, bringing my water bottle back with me into the kitchen.

Ariana handed me another cupcake when I returned to the table.

I took a bite and focused on comparing it to the others I'd tasted. So far, cupcake number two was still my winner. We all tried the rest of the cupcake batches and agreed. The second cupcake was the best, and it'd be on the menu this fall, topped with honey cinnamon frosting.

"That was awesome," I told Ariana as everyone else got back to work. "Do you come up with new flavors a lot?"

"We try to add a few new ones each season."

I thought of how cool it would be to come up with my own recipe. I'd only ever baked using other people's recipes. But if I got onto *Kids Bake Challenge!* I'd have to bake from my own memory.

I *should come up with my own new cupcake flavor.* If Ariana liked it, maybe she'd add it to her menu. She'd definitely give me a positive evaluation at the end of this internship if I gave her a new flavor recipe—and I could use it for my *Kids Bake Challenge!* audition. Maybe Ariana would even let me film my audition video in the shop's kitchen.

For the next half hour, Ariana had me go through a shipment of strawberries and pick out all of the rotten ones. It was super boring compared to taste-testing cupcakes, but I didn't mind too much. I started imagining possible cupcake recipes, listing all sorts of random ingredients in my head. *Kumquats. Rhubarb. Cranberries. Hazelnuts. Kiwi.*

This wouldn't be easy, but I couldn't wait to get started.

Chapter Thirteen

I was searching for more ingredients and cupcake inspiration pictures on my computer when Grandma knocked on my bedroom door and peeked inside. "I have to return my book to the library," she said. "Do you want to come and get something?"

"Okay. I can look at the cookbooks." I grabbed my backpack and threw my journal inside.

When we walked into the library fifteen minutes later, Grandma said, "I'm going to see what's new in the mystery section. Want to meet back here in an hour?"

"Sounds good." I gave her a quick wave and walked to the cookbook section, which was on the main floor.

I'd stood in front of those shelves so many times before. I pulled a few baking cookbooks down and sat at a table to flip through them. The recipes all sounded really good. Now I wanted to make peanut butter banana pudding and "Everything but the Kitchen Sink" cookies filled with crushed-up pretzels, chocolate chips, toffee bits, and nuts. But seeing pictures and descriptions of completed recipes wasn't helping me think of new ones. Maybe I needed to walk around the supermarket instead.

I carefully put the cookbooks back on the shelf and checked the time on my phone. I still had forty-five minutes before I had to meet Grandma.

I could start writing a letter back to Marcus, since I had my journal with me. But I still didn't know how to respond to his last letter.

An idea came to me. My sixth-grade social studies teacher once instructed us to use only library books to complete one of our projects. We couldn't use the internet at all. It was the first time I'd used only the library to research something. Dad ended up helping me.

I walked to the information desk.

"Excuse me?" I asked the librarian, who was staring down at something. When she looked up, I realized she wasn't an actual librarian. Or at least, she didn't seem old enough to be one. She was white with wavy brown hair, and she wore a gray Smith College T-shirt. Maybe she was still a college student, working at the library for the summer.

She glanced up at me, and then said, "Children's floor is down the stairs to your right."

"I know that," I said. "I'm looking for books about crimes."

"The children's librarian downstairs can help you with that."

"I'm not looking for children's books," I said, a little more forcefully. "I want the grown-up books about crimes."

For a second, she looked like she was about to question why a middle schooler wanted to look at adult crime books. "Fiction or nonfiction?"

"Uh, nonfiction," I said.

"That's upstairs." She turned to a laminated map of the library on the desk in front of her. "The true crime section is to the right. The criminal law section is behind it."

"Thank you!" I turned toward the stairs and forced myself not to run all the way up them.

When I got upstairs, I realized I'd never stepped foot on that floor before. But as the girl had said, the true crime section was to the right. I walked into the stacks, not really knowing what book I was looking for. What I wanted to know was if it was really possible for an innocent person to go to prison. I had no idea if the answer to that was in a book, but there was only one way to find out.

People were scattered around the nonfiction floor of the library, some looking through books and others sitting at tables reading. It was very quiet, much quieter than the main floor and children's floor. Everyone seemed very serious. Nobody was in the true crime section, which was a relief. I didn't want any adults questioning why I was there.

I walked up and down the shelves, staring at book titles until my eyes blurred. There were a bunch of books on serial killers—not at all what I was looking for. I started to worry I wouldn't find what I needed and was about to give up. But finally, at the end of the row, one book's title caught my eye. It was called *The Wrongfully Convicted*. The cover had a grid of square photos, like an online photo album, but each picture showed a different person's face looking at the camera. They were all men, and most of them were Black. Like Marcus. I slipped it off the shelf and carried it to a nearby empty table.

I sat down and cracked open the book, reading through the table of contents. Then I skimmed the introduction, which was written by some lawyer guy. He worked for an organization called the Innocence Project, which he explained helped innocent people get out of prison.

Did this mean Marcus could be telling the truth? If that kind of organization existed, then innocent people must go to prison. I couldn't believe it.

The rest of the chapters were about different cases, so I turned to the first one and started to read.

It described how one man went to prison for armed robbery, but more than one person said they saw him somewhere else, not at the crime scene. He didn't actually commit the crime. Still, in the end, the jury didn't believe his side of the story. He was sentenced to prison for twenty years. He had to leave his family, a wife and two kids.

He had an alibi like Marcus. But he still went to prison.

I read on. Years later, the man wrote a letter to the Innocence Project, and they agreed to help him. They got DNA evidence from the crime scene tested again, and the results showed it didn't belong to this guy. He really was innocent. The Innocence Project got him out of prison.

"Wow," I said out loud before remembering I was in the quietest room ever. I flipped through the rest of the book, where there were at least a dozen other stories like that one, of people who had spent years in prison until the Innocence Project took on their cases and helped them get out. Now they were all free.

There was a page in the book with graphs and numbers. It showed how many people the Innocence Project helped get out of prison, which was in the hundreds. I couldn't believe that many innocent people were convicted. I stared at another chart that showed the different races of the people the Innocence Project helped. Most of them were Black.

Of course. I knew about the Black Lives Matter movement, how Black people all over the country were getting shot by police for no good reason. If those police officers weren't going to jail, then it made sense that the whole prison system was messed up. I never thought about whether prisons had the wrong people before. I assumed that if you committed a crime, you got the punishment you deserved, and innocent people would always be proven innocent. Apparently not.

I opened my journal and wrote down the name of the book. I couldn't take it home; I didn't want one more thing to hide from my parents. But I had to be able to look it up again later. Underneath the book's title, I wrote down "the Innocence Project." I needed to research them more.

I was about to get up to use a computer when somebody sat down at the table across from me. It must have been one of the other grown-ups on the floor, and I kept my head down as I figured out how to explain what I was doing there. But when I looked up, it wasn't a grown-up staring at me.

It was Trevor.

Chapter Fourteen

"Whatcha reading?" Trevor asked, smiling.

"Shhh! What are you doing here?" I looked past Trevor, but thankfully, he wasn't with either of his parents.

"I was gonna ask you the same thing," he said. "Simon dropped me off at the library so I could return my book and get another one. When I walked in, I saw you come up the stairs. I thought it was weird, since the kids' books and cookbooks are downstairs."

"So you followed me." Why did he keep butting his head where it didn't belong?

"No," Trevor said. "I went down to the kids' floor first, and got my book." He held up the book he'd chosen—*Ghost*, by Jason Reynolds. "And then I came up here to find you. Are you hiding from someone?"

"Who would I be hiding from?" I asked, as if it was the most ridiculous question ever. I closed *The Wrongfully Convicted*, ready to get up and away from Trevor.

He shrugged. "I dunno. It's weird that you're up here." Then he caught a glimpse of the book on the table. As he stared at it, his face twisted in confusion. I could almost see the wheels in his brain turning. "Wait, does this have something to do with your dad in prison?"

"Um . . ." I stalled. I didn't want to talk to Trevor. I wasn't sure I could trust him. But I was dying to talk about what I'd just learned. And he did already know about Marcus . . .

"Does it?" Trevor asked again.

Just like that, the story started spilling out of me. I told Trevor about everything between Marcus's first letter arriving on my birthday up until the letter where Marcus said he was innocent. It was like my brain short-circuited and I forgot who I was talking to, that I was still mad at Trevor. I was so caught up in how excited I was to have found information that showed Marcus could be telling the truth.

"Wow." Trevor looked at me in awe. "I can't believe you've been writing to your birth dad in prison. In secret."

I looked at him and realized what I'd just done. "I shouldn't have told you all that." Panic started to balloon in my chest. "You can't tell anyone what I said. Promise."

"Yeah. Okay."

"You didn't promise," I said. "I mean it. You can't tell anyone. It's really important."

Trevor's face became serious. "I promise." And then he looked at me funny. "Since when are you a rebel?"

"I'm not," I said, though when I thought about it, it was sort of true. It was so unlike me—lying to my parents, sneaking around doing something they wouldn't approve of. I never lied to them this much about anything, and I felt a little guilty.

But now that I knew Marcus might be innocent, there was no way I could stop.

Maybe I could track down Marcus's lawyer and ask him questions about the case. Or I could find his alibi witness and listen to their side of the story. If that person really did see Marcus when the crime was happening, then I would know for sure whether he was telling the truth.

If I could prove that Marcus didn't commit his crime, then Mom would have to let me have a relationship with him. Then the lying could stop for good.

"If he's innocent, then how come he's been in prison this whole time?" Trevor asked.

I hesitated, not sure if I should trust Trevor with anything else. Would he really keep my secret?

"What?" Trevor asked, as if my thoughts were written all over my face. "I'm not going to tell anybody."

"Okay," I finally said. "Marcus said he had an alibi—like, he was somewhere else when the crime happened."

"Wait, for real?" Trevor asked.

I nodded and put my hand on the book. "Then I found this—it has all these stories about innocent people who went to prison. I didn't think that happened."

"I guess I knew that," Trevor said. "My parents have all of these talks with me—like, because I'm Black, I have to be extra careful around the police. Stuff like that."

"My mom had that talk with me, too," I said. "I hadn't made the connection."

I told Trevor about the Innocence Project and filled him in on the case I read about. I still couldn't believe how unfair it was. What was the point of a legal system if it didn't work a lot of the time? And what about all the people who didn't know to ask for the Innocence Project's help?

"That's messed up," Trevor said.

"I know," I said. "I'm going to go use a computer and see what I can find about Marcus's case."

"Cool, let's go," Trevor said as he pushed his chair back.

"What do you mean, 'let's'?" I asked.

"I want to come, too," Trevor said. "I'm curious now."

"Um . . ." I hesitated, not sure if I was ready to be friends with Trevor again. But it was nice to talk all of this through with him. It was almost like before.

"Okay, then," I finally said.

I left *The Wrongfully Convicted* on the table, gathered my other stuff, and then Trevor and I walked to the nearest computer.

My mom never told me any of the details of the crime—only that the victim was someone Marcus knew in college. I didn't want to look it up before, because I was sort of scared of what I'd find. But now that I wanted to figure out if he was really innocent, I needed to know exactly what happened the day of the crime.

I typed "Marcus Johnson" into the search bar, and the page filled with links and pictures of some jazz musician. I had to get more specific, so I put "Malden" after his name, since that's where he and my mom grew up.

A few articles from over twelve years earlier popped up at the top of the list. In the middle of the page, a few images appeared. I immediately recognized Marcus in one of them.

I clicked on it to get a better look. The picture showed his head and the top of his shoulders, with a gray background. It had to be Marcus's mug shot.

"That's him." The only other picture I'd seen of Marcus was him smiling at the basketball game. But in this one, Marcus looked mean—like a murderer would look. His jaw was tight, his eyes stony, as if he didn't feel bad at all.

I started to panic; maybe this was all a mistake—he was guilty, of course he was guilty. But then I looked at the picture a little closer and noticed something else in his eyes. It seemed like maybe he was putting up a front, like he was really frightened but trying not to show it.

I wasn't sure which was right.

It looked like the picture came from an article, so I clicked on it. I leaned even closer to the computer screen and started to read.

Arrest Made in UMass Student's Murder
Published: Friday, November 1

A suspect has been charged today in the death of 18-year-old Lucy Hernandez, authorities said. The University of Massachusetts freshman was found dead in her apartment near campus on Sunday morning. Marcus Johnson, 18, UMass freshman and Malden resident, is charged with first degree murder.

Hernandez's roommate found her body in her apartment the morning of October 27. Authorities ruled the death a homicide later that day, a Sunday. An autopsy determined that the cause of Hernandez's death was blunt force trauma to her head, according to the prosecutor's office. The coroner estimated that her death occurred sometime between 3:00 and 5:00 p.m. on October 26.

Authorities said Hernandez and Johnson knew each other through school, and classmates believed the two were dating. A witness reported seeing Johnson exit Hernandez's apartment building the afternoon of her death.

Suddenly, it was hard to breathe. What happened to Lucy was so horrible. I couldn't read any more.

"He sounds guilty," Trevor said.

"I know," I said. "But maybe the witness got it wrong. Maybe this was all a misunderstanding."

"Maybe," Trevor said, but he didn't sound too convinced.

I went back to the search results and clicked on the next article. That headline read, "UMass Student Murder Suspect in Court." This article had more pictures.

In one, Marcus was wearing an orange jumpsuit with handcuffs holding his hands in front of him, and a police officer walked beside him. It was hard not to see him as a criminal when he was in that jumpsuit. In the photo, his eyes were pointed toward the floor, and hair dotted his chin and upper lip, like he hadn't gotten to shave. This is probably what he looked like right now, only older. Maybe he even had a full mustache and beard now.

In a low voice, I read a few lines of the article. "Marcus Johnson faced a judge in court today. The eighteen-year-old is accused of murdering his former classmate Lucy Hernandez in October."

Lucy's picture was in the article, too. The way she was posed, and with the blue fading background, it looked like a yearbook photo. Her wavy brown hair flowed past her shoulders, and she wore a black sweater, silver dangly earrings, and a silver necklace with a key charm. I wondered who gave her the necklace, and if it meant anything. She looked happy in the picture, probably excited to be graduating from high school.

She was alive, and then she wasn't. I swallowed hard as my stomach churned.

"You look like you're gonna throw up," Trevor said.

"It's just . . . that's her," I said.

"Yeah. She was pretty."

I stared at her picture for a few more seconds, memorizing her features. "I know."

Then I forced myself to go back to the article. It said Marcus pleaded "not guilty." There was a picture of Marcus standing next to his lawyer, Anthony Miller. He was white, shorter than Marcus, and had a bald spot on the top of his head. His gray suit and tie made him look like a lawyer, plus the way he stood there with his hands clasped in front of him, all serious, as he focused on the judge.

I glanced at the clock on the bottom right of the computer screen. "I have to go back downstairs and meet my grandmother in a minute."

"Okay," Trevor said. "I guess I'll head back to the kids' floor."

We got up and went down to the library's main floor. I couldn't believe we were walking together, like we were friends again.

"I won't tell anybody anything," Trevor said. "I can help you, if you want, with whatever you're doing with Marcus."

"Maybe."

We said goodbye, and Trevor skipped down the steps to the children's floor.

I made my way to the circulation desk, where I found Grandma holding a couple of mystery novels.

She looked at my empty hands. "You didn't find anything to check out?"

I shook my head. "Not this time."

When Grandma was done checking out her books, we walked toward the library's entrance. I thought about what the articles said. They made Marcus sound guilty, even though he said he was innocent. But Grandma said things aren't as simple as black-and-white. What if the truth wasn't either?

Chapter Fifteen

An hour after Grandma and I got home, I heard the familiar squeaky sound of Trevor's storm door. He was back from the library.

Talking to Trevor at the library felt so normal, like we'd never gotten in a fight at all. It was a relief to be able to talk out loud about Marcus with somebody other than Grandma.

I went outside, Butternut following behind me. I found Trevor sitting on his side of the porch steps, holding his new library book.

"Hey." I sat down across from him, on my side of the steps. Butternut found a patch of sun and lay down on it.

"What's up?" Trevor flashed a quick smile.

"How was the rest of the library?" I asked.

"Good. I hung out on the computers after you left."

"Nice."

After a long pause, I said, "I'm ready to tell you why I've been mad at you."

Trevor put his book down. "Okay."

I took a deep breath. "It started when you joined the basketball team." That was at the beginning of the sixth grade, last year. Trevor had always said that he wanted to join the team when he got to middle school, and that's exactly what he did.

"You're mad that I joined the team?" Trevor asked. "You knew I was going to."

"I didn't think you'd start ignoring me."

"I didn't," he said.

"Yes, you did. You didn't talk to me as much at school."

"I couldn't," he said. "I had to talk to the guys on the team, too. And you were hanging out with Maya and Jasmine. You were the one ignoring me."

"What are you talking about?" I asked.

"During the summer, it's always the two of us. But when school starts, you go back to Jasmine and Maya, and it's like I don't matter to you anymore."

Wow. Was that really how Trevor felt? I did spend a lot of time with Jasmine and Maya during the school year, since we didn't see each other during the summer, but that didn't mean I didn't care about Trevor. "You still mattered," I mumbled.

"It didn't feel like it," Trevor said.

"Well, what about you?" I asked, remembering why I was out there in the first place. "You've been pretending to be my friend this whole time."

Trevor looked up at me, his face a big question mark. He had no idea what I was talking about.

I took another deep breath. "I heard you guys. Last month."

"Heard who?"

"You, Sean, and Lincoln. You were here on the porch after school. I was sick, so I stayed home all day. I was in the living room and the window was open, so I could hear everything. You guys couldn't see me because I was lying on the couch."

I remembered the huge pile of used tissues that littered the coffee table, and how Butternut stayed near me the whole day, like he knew I was sick and needed a friend. I was in a cold-medicine haze when Trevor's and the other boys' voices woke me up. But I heard them loud and clear.

"Zoe Washington lives on the other side of this house, right?" It was Sean's voice, which I recognized right away since he had a thick Boston accent. When he said my name, it sounded like "Waaah-shington."

I didn't dare move from my position on the couch, so they wouldn't know I was right on the other side of the window from them.

"Yeah," Trevor said.

"What's with her?" Sean asked. I couldn't see his face, but I could picture him scowling.

"What do you mean?" Trevor asked.

"Why'd she have to tell Mr. Peters that I started that fight with Will?" Sean asked. "I didn't even start it."

Trevor didn't say a word.

"Yeah, why'd she have to open her big mouth about it?" Lincoln asked. "Nobody asked her."

"Exactly," Sean said. "She thinks she's better than everyone, but she's really a loser."

Then Lincoln asked, "Did you hear what she did in gym class one time? She fell when we were playing basketball. I was there. She tripped over nothing—her own feet. She looked ridiculous. But then later I tripped her on purpose and she fell again."

"Oh yeah, that was wicked funny!" Sean said.

I heard laughter. There were definitely more than two voices in the mix, and Trevor's laugh was unmistakable.

My eyes stung with tears, and there was no holding them back.

"It sucks that you have to live right next to her," Sean said. "It's gotta be so annoying to hear her whiny voice every day, right?"

"Uh . . ." Trevor paused for a second and I waited for him to say no, and that I was his best friend.

But instead, he said, "Yeah, I guess." There was a pause, and then he said, "We're not really friends. We hang out sometimes during the summer, when I have nothing better to do."

It was a punch to my gut. I got up and ran to my room, burying myself under my covers while I sobbed.

All this time, I thought Trevor was one of my best friends. But I'd been wrong.

I recapped all of this to Trevor, who now stared at me with a pained expression on his face. "I had no idea you heard that," he said. "I didn't mean it, any of it. I was mad at you because you were always with Jasmine and Maya. And I didn't know what to say when those guys asked. But it's not true."

"I only told Mr. Peters about the fight because he asked me what I saw," I said. "I didn't want to lie to him."

Trevor nodded.

"Nobody forced you to hang out with me," I said, my voice cracking. "You didn't have to do me any favors."

"I didn't," Trevor said. "I like hanging out with you. A lot. The summer is always my favorite. You're my best friend. I'm really sorry."

"If that's true, why would you let those guys say that stuff about me?" I asked.

"I don't know." Trevor paused and glanced down at his sneakers. "I wanted to fit in, I guess. It was wrong."

I wanted to accept his apology and forget it all happened. Get back to our friendship and summer adventures like nothing had changed.

But it was like when you drew something in pencil and then tried to erase it—the pencil lines would mostly go away, but sometimes the indent would still be there, so you could still sort of see what had been erased. That's how Trevor's apology felt—like he was trying to erase my pain by saying he was sorry, but he couldn't make it all disappear.

"Do you believe me?" Trevor swallowed hard.

"I keep remembering what you said." *We're not really friends.* "I need more time to get over it."

Trevor nodded.

"Guess I'll see you later." I got up from the porch steps.

"Later," Trevor said. His mouth turned up in a small smile.

Maybe the pencil marks couldn't be erased, but at some point, you could decide to turn to a new page.

"Do anything interesting today?" Dad asked me during dinner that night.

"Not really," I lied, and chewed on a piece of asparagus.

"How has your internship been going?" Mom asked.

"Good."

"What kinds of things have you been doing?" she asked.

"I don't want to talk about it right now," I said. What I really wanted to talk about was Marcus, but if I brought him up, Mom would just shut me down again.

"All right," Mom said. She started talking to Dad about something that happened at work, and I stopped paying attention.

I ate a couple more bites of salmon and rice, and then asked to be excused.

Back in my room with the door closed, I searched for more information about Marcus and his case, but the other articles I found repeated the same stuff I already knew. None of them mentioned anything about an alibi witness. I even searched for Marcus's name with the words "alibi witness" after it, in case I missed it somewhere, but no real results came up. Why was that?

I needed to know if Marcus was telling me the truth. If he was, I could keep writing to him and keep getting to know him. But if he *was* lying about this, then I couldn't trust him.

For the longest time, I didn't care whether or not I knew my birth father. I had my parents, and they were all I needed. But his letters were making me realize that there had always been a piece of me missing, like a chunk of my heart. I was finally filling in that hole. Marcus seemed to care about me. He actually wanted to know about my life. And he liked cooking! I probably got my love of baking from him. What else could I have inherited from him? I wanted to find out.

There was only one way I could think of to know whether or not he was really innocent, and that was to find the alibi witness. If I could find the person who was with Marcus when Lucy was killed, and could prove it, then I would be able to believe that he really didn't do it. And that he was who he said he was.

I'd find Marcus's alibi witness—and the truth.

Chapter Sixteen

There was one person who knew all of the details of Marcus's case, and maybe even the alibi witness's name— Anthony Miller, Marcus's lawyer. When I searched online for his name, I found a website with a list of public defenders. Mr. Miller's name was on the list. I read through the website and figured out that he was assigned to Marcus because Marcus couldn't afford his own lawyer.

The contact page only listed a general email address and phone number for the law office. I sent an email to the general address, asking for information about the case, about an alibi witness. Anything that might prove

Marcus was really innocent. I didn't mention that I was a twelve-year-old.

Now I needed to write Marcus and tell him about my plan. I opened my desk drawer and took out my stationery.

From the Desk of Zoe Washington

July 27

Dear Marcus,

How are you? I'm good. I can't believe summer is already halfway over!

I'm sorry it took me a while to write back. When I read your last letter, I thought you were lying to me. I didn't think innocent people went to prison. But now I know that it does happen. I really want to believe you, but I barely know you. I haven't even heard your voice before. So how am I supposed to know for sure? I thought of one way. Can you tell me the name of the alibi witness? Then I could find them and hear their side of the story. If I could do that, and they said they remembered you from the day of the crime, I'd feel so much better. Though I'd feel sad that you've been in prison all this time for no reason.

> Have you heard of the Innocence Project? I read about them at the library. If you're really innocent, maybe they could get you out of prison.

I paused writing and got out Marcus's last letter from my backpack. I uncrumpled it and smoothed it out, then reread it. The last song he'd sent was "Water Runs Dry," by Boyz II Men, so I played it on my phone and picked up my pen again.

> I'm listening to the Boyz II Men song right now. Wow—their voices are so good. This might be my favorite on my Little Tomato playlist so far. Send more, please!
>
> I can't believe you like to cook! What's your favorite recipe? Do you know one of your mom's recipes by heart? Maybe I can try to make it myself. That's so cool that you get to work in the kitchen at the prison. I guess I thought you stayed in a cell all day. Do you get to do anything else?
>
> My baking internship is going well. I decided to make up a totally new cupcake recipe, so maybe Ariana will sell it at her shop. Can you think of a unique ingredient that would be good in a cupcake?

I thought of something—it was possible Marcus had never seen a picture of me. I found an extra wallet-sized print of my sixth-grade photo in my desk drawer. I didn't always like my school photos, but that one had turned out pretty good. I liked the purple sweater I was wearing, and my half-up, half-down hairstyle looked nice. I'd put extra shea butter hair cream on it so my curls wouldn't frizz.

> Here's my recent school picture. I thought you might like to see what I look like now.
> Write back soon,
> Zoe

I put the letter in its envelope and stuck it back in my hiding spot. Tomorrow, I'd give it to Grandma to mail.

I got up to grab a glass of water from the kitchen. But then something else gnawed at me.

It was my school photo—it reminded me of Lucy Hernandez's picture from the article. I hadn't looked her up before, but now I wanted to know more about her.

I opened my computer again and searched for her name. I skimmed the results, and they were all articles about how Lucy had died. It was awful; when you looked up a person, you were supposed to see stories about their life, not their terrible death.

Then I found a memorial page for her. It was a really simple website, with a few photos of her on top. In one, she wore a cheerleading uniform, and another showed her with a bunch of other cheerleaders on a football field. Below the photos was an area where her friends and family could post messages. Some of them were in Spanish. As I read through them, my eyes filled with tears. People loved her a whole lot, and she seemed like a really nice person. I thought about how I'd feel if anything happened to Jasmine or Maya, or Trevor, and my throat clenched up. Lucy didn't deserve to die.

If Marcus was guilty, why did he do it?

I hoped with every inch of my heart that Marcus wasn't responsible, that this was all a big mistake.

When I handed Grandma my letter to mail the next day, it hit me: she was around when Marcus was arrested, and when he had his trial. Maybe she knew stuff about the case that I couldn't find online. Like why none of the articles mentioned his alibi or a witness.

"Grandma, can I ask you something?"

"Of course," she said.

I took a deep breath. "In his last letter, when Marcus told me he's innocent, were you surprised?" I knew she'd read it before she gave it to me.

"Well, he told me he was going to tell you that."

"He did?"

"Yes," Grandma said. "I know I'm going behind your parents' back to let you write to him, but I still want to keep you safe. I wrote to him and asked him to call me so we could talk about him writing to you."

"You talked to him on the phone?" I was dying to know what Marcus's voice sounded like.

Grandma nodded. "It was a quick phone call. He couldn't stay on long. But it was long enough for me to make sure that he isn't trying to hurt you in any way."

"Oh."

After a few moments of silence, Grandma asked, "Is there something else you want to know?"

"Oh, yeah. Hold on." I ran to my room to grab my journal. When I got back to the living room, I sat next to Grandma on the couch. I opened to all the notes I'd taken about Marcus's case and the Innocence Project.

"Marcus told me he had an alibi," I said. "But I couldn't find anything online about it. Do you think he's telling the truth?"

"He told me the same thing after he was arrested," Grandma said. "Here. Let me grab a cup of tea, and then I'll tell you what I know."

Chapter Seventeen

"*After Marcus was arrested,*" Grandma began once she was back and settled on the couch with a mug of green ginger tea, "I visited him at the prison a couple of times before he went on trial. Your mom didn't want to see him, but I had to. I had to look him in the eyes and hear what happened in his own words. That's when he told me about his alibi."

"What was it?" I asked.

"He was at a tag sale," Grandma said.

"For real? Like at somebody's house?"

Grandma nodded. "He said he saw some ad online and emailed the lady before going over there."

"Why wasn't she part of the trial?" I asked. "None of the articles I found talked about her."

"Marcus's lawyer never brought her to court."

I scrunched my eyebrows. "Why not?"

"The lawyer never even looked for her." Grandma sipped her tea.

In the letter, Marcus only said his lawyer couldn't prove his innocence, not that he never looked for the alibi witness. It didn't make any sense. "Why not? She could've told everyone that Marcus was somewhere else when the crime took place."

"Exactly," Grandma said. "She could've really helped Marcus's case. But, you know, he didn't have the money to pay for a big-shot lawyer after he was arrested. He had to use the defense lawyer assigned to him for free. And this lawyer . . ." She shook her head. "To me, it was like he didn't care one bit about what happened to Marcus."

"Why not?" I asked. "Didn't he want to win the case?"

Grandma exhaled. "He got paid either way, so I'm not sure it mattered. He seemed completely biased against Marcus. He wanted him to plead guilty, and take a deal, but Marcus refused."

"What do you mean by 'biased'?" I asked.

"I think he saw a Black man being charged with murder, and saw no reason to believe he was actually innocent,"

Grandma explained. "He went through the motions of defending him in court without putting in any real work."

"That's terrible!" I huffed.

Grandma nodded.

I thought of my email to Mr. Miller, and wondered what he'd say when he replied. If he replied at all.

"Do you think Marcus is really innocent?" I asked.

Grandma put her mug down on the coffee table. "Yes. I do."

I blinked at her, surprised by how confident she sounded. "You do?"

"Yes," Grandma repeated. "Marcus dated your mom for two years, and I got to know him pretty well. He never seemed like a violent person. He was always so polite and respectful. And such a gentleman to your mom. You could tell he really respected her." She laughed. "Your mom would take forever to get ready for dates. She'd be in that bathroom singing along to some song, putting on makeup or whatever. Anyway, instead of waiting outside in the car, Marcus would come inside and talk to your granddad and me. He talked about college. Said he wanted to travel. One time he helped your granddad fix the leaky pipe under the sink while he waited for Natalie to get ready. He got his shirt all dirty, so he had to run back home and get a new one."

"Wow," I said.

"There's this quote from Maya Angelou," Grandma said. "'When someone shows you who they are, believe them.' That quote usually refers to when someone shows you their bad side, but I think it's also true when someone shows you how good they are. I really do think Marcus is a good person. I don't see how he was capable of killing someone. I always trust my gut, and my gut has always said to believe him."

I nodded, feeling a little more hopeful.

"Then I don't get it," I said. "Why did the court think he could've killed somebody?"

"The prosecutor told this one story about Marcus . . . ," Grandma began, but then shook her head. "Never mind."

"What? You have to tell me."

Grandma exhaled again. "There was one time when Marcus was a senior. He got into a fistfight with another player at a basketball game."

"What happened?" I asked.

"The other player provoked Marcus—got him mad enough to fight. Your granddad wasn't too happy when he heard about this, so the next time he saw Marcus, he asked him for an explanation. Marcus said that the other player, who was white, called him the N-word while they were playing. Under his breath, when nobody else could hear him."

I knew exactly what word she meant. Mom and Grandma had talked to me about it. Racist people used it. And sometimes other Black people called each other that, which wasn't racist but wasn't great. My parents had told me that I should never use that word, and to tell them if anyone ever called me that. I'd never heard anyone say it about me.

"When the white kid called Marcus that," Grandma said, "Marcus got really mad. Of course he did. So that's what started the fight. A lot of people were at the game, and they all saw it. The white kid, he was the star player of the other team, so a lot of people took his side. With all the racism around Boston, people weren't about to take a Black kid's word over a white kid's."

Every once in a while, I'd overhear my parents talk about how racist Boston was. I noticed it myself, too. Like all the times people gave Dad and me "the look." Once, I went to a fancy clothing store on Newbury Street with Mom, and a saleslady started following us around the store, looking at us like she didn't trust us with the merchandise. As soon as Mom noticed what was going on, she pulled me out of the store. "I'm not giving them my business," she'd told me.

I had no idea where the idea of Black people as thieves

came from, but it wasn't the first time something like that had happened. In fourth grade, a girl told me that I wasn't invited to her birthday party because her parents said Black people steal. I'd said her parents didn't know what they were talking about. After I told my mom, she stopped herself from cursing out loud, and said she didn't want me going to that racist family's house anyway.

"Did Marcus say what the other kid called him?" I asked Grandma.

"Nobody else heard it. But I believed him, and your granddad did too." She paused and then said, "Anyway, when Marcus was later accused of the crime, the prosecutors told that story, used it against him. They said he had a violent past."

"But getting into a fight isn't the same thing as killing someone!" I squeezed a corner of a pillow between my fingers. "And the other kid called him the N-word!"

"I know. But it was up to the jury, and they decided that Marcus was capable of all kinds of violence, even the worst kind." She sighed. "People look at someone like Marcus—a tall, strong, dark-skinned boy—and they make assumptions about him. Even if it isn't right. The jury, the judge, the public, even his own lawyer—they all assumed Marcus must be guilty because he's Black. It's all part of systemic racism."

"It's not fair."

"I know, baby," Grandma said, her expression sad.

I thought about all of this. "Why didn't Mom want to see him in prison before the trial?"

"She was really mad at him."

"Why?" I asked.

"Because Marcus was friends with the victim."

"Lucy," I said.

"That's right." Grandma said. "Marcus and Lucy were spending a lot of time together, because they were in the same study group. Your mom thought something more was going on. Marcus said there wasn't, but your mom, she had her doubts. It was tough for them—he stayed in Boston for college, and she went down to New York. It wasn't a huge distance, but it was still hard on their relationship."

I nodded, remembering how I'd read that some people even thought Marcus and Lucy were dating before she died.

"Your mom wanted to believe he was innocent, but when the prosecution brought a witness into court who said he'd seen Marcus leaving Lucy's place around the time of the murder, she started having doubts. I did too, to be honest, but Marcus insisted that it wasn't him. Eyewitnesses get it wrong all the time."

Grandma continued. "Plus, the crime happened after your mom found out she was pregnant with you." She poked my nose, like she used to do when I was a little kid, and I smiled for a second.

"She was so mad at Marcus," Grandma said. "For spending time with that girl in the first place. For getting arrested and leaving her alone, when she was already scared about having a baby so young. The whole mess broke her heart. Then he was convicted, and I think she decided it was easier to believe he did it, let him go, and move on."

When Grandma explained it like that, I felt some sympathy for Mom. It must've been really hard for her.

"Do you think Marcus could get out of prison, if we found his witness?" I asked Grandma.

"I don't know." She put her hand on top of mine. "I'm telling you all of this because you deserve to hear the truth. But I don't want you to get wrapped up in it. You're only a kid. Even if Marcus is innocent, the chances of him getting out are slim. Who knows where this woman is? And getting a new lawyer would be expensive, too."

But I wasn't only a kid. And just because it wasn't easy didn't mean it couldn't get done. Dad had always told me that when I had a hard time on a school project. And he was always right. Sometimes that homework wasn't easy at all, but I always got it done. Most of the time, I got a better grade on it than I expected.

"If Marcus really didn't do it," I said, my voice solemn, "then it means somebody else did. That person should be in prison, not Marcus."

Grandma put her arm around my shoulder and squeezed. "You're right. This isn't only about Marcus. It's also about justice for Lucy. That poor girl's family deserves to see her actual murderer behind bars."

"Do you think there's any chance Marcus can get out of prison, and they'll find the real murderer?"

"There's always hope," Grandma said. "But that doesn't mean it's enough to make change. I've followed Marcus's case, and he tried to appeal the verdict a few months later, but his appeal was denied. At this point, if Marcus is innocent, he needs more than hope to get out of prison anytime soon—he needs a miracle."

A miracle.

I had a lot of work ahead of me.

Chapter Eighteen

I spent the next couple of days looking up more facts about wrongful convictions, and found out that the Innocence Project had an office in Boston. Their website said you could send a letter to request assistance. I thought about writing to them, but decided to wait until after I'd tracked down Marcus's alibi witness.

On Sunday night after dinner, I browsed the internet some more. One article said that thousands of innocent people were convicted of crimes each year. I couldn't believe the number was that high.

Another article said Black people were more likely to be wrongfully convicted of murder. If this was known, then why wasn't more being done to fix it? Probably because not enough people cared, like Grandma said. A lump formed in my throat.

But then I read that the year before, a record number of innocent people were freed from prison. So, there was hope.

I closed my laptop as soon as I heard a knock on my bedroom door. Dad peeked inside my room. "Get your shoes on and meet me at the car in five minutes."

I groaned. "What if I don't want to?"

"Too bad," Dad said, all serious. But then he smiled. "But you're going to want to."

He shut my door again, and I stared at my closed laptop for a few moments. It was already eight o'clock at night, so whatever it was probably wouldn't take long. I left my room, slipped into my flip-flops next to the front door, and went outside.

Our car was running in the driveway, with Dad in the driver's seat and Mom next to him. I got into the back seat and put my seat belt on, crossing my arms on top of it.

Dad started driving while I stared out the window, zoning out to his favorite jazz station on the radio. The sun was setting, and it was as if someone had taken a brush with pink paint and made a streak across the sky, which was pale blue but getting darker by the minute. I guessed where we were going by the route we were taking. Five minutes later, Dad drove into Davis Square. He found a metered spot, and once he parked, we all got out of the car.

We automatically started walking toward the center of Davis, straight to J.P. Licks. Home of the best ice cream in Boston.

We walked inside the small shop and got in line. I stared at all of the flavors on the chalkboard menu, and decided on peanut butter cookies 'n' cream in a waffle cone. Dad ordered a cup with one scoop of coffee ice cream and one scoop of maple walnut. Mom got a cone with a scoop of coconut almond chip.

We didn't say anything as Dad paid for our ice creams, or while he grabbed way too many napkins, like every other time we'd gone there. Mom picked up a spoon even though she had a cone. Then we went outside and found an empty bench in the square.

I stared ahead at all of the people walking around Davis and licked my ice cream before it could melt all over me.

"So, when are you going to tell us more about your internship?" Dad asked me.

I shrugged.

"Ari says you're doing a great job so far." Mom smiled and licked her ice cream.

I nodded, suppressing my own smile. Kids Bake Challenge! *audition, here I come.*

"C'mon, Zoe. Talk to us," Dad said, gently nudging me with his shoulder.

I turned to Mom. "I want to write a letter to Marcus."

Mom looked taken aback. "What? We talked about this."

"But you're not letting me have a say."

Her mouth formed a straight line. She glanced at Dad before looking at me again. "Because you're not ready to have a say."

"I disagree," I said.

"Why don't we talk about this when we get home," Dad said.

I ignored him and asked Mom, "Why are you so scared of me writing to him?"

"I'm not scared," Mom said. "I'm concerned."

"Why?"

"He's a convicted murderer."

Convicted, yes. But guilty? Maybe not.

"Do you really think he did it?" I asked.

"Did what?" Mom asked.

"Do you really think Marcus killed someone? He said he was innocent. During the trial," I quickly added.

"How do you know that?" she asked.

"Um . . ." I thought fast. "I looked him up online. I was curious about him. I read that he pleaded 'not guilty' before the trial."

"You can't trust him. He's—"

"How do you know?" I asked. "Do you really think he could kill someone?"

Mom looked down at her ice cream. Finally, she said, "I didn't want to believe it at first. But I was at the trial and I heard all the testimony. Marcus was the last person seen with Lucy."

"What if that witness got it wrong?"

"He lied to me about hanging out with her at all. I couldn't trust him anymore." She paused and then said, "I don't know. Maybe he didn't mean to do it, but I still think he could've."

"But you don't know for sure!"

"You're right," Mom said. "But I have to go with my gut on this."

Grandma had said the same thing about her gut. Except she believed Marcus.

I turned to Dad. "What do you think?"

He thought about it. "I know this stinks. But I think your mom knows what's best for you."

All of a sudden, I felt trapped, sitting on that bench between the two of them. I stood up.

Mom stood up too, and her voice got louder. "Zoe, I'm only trying to protect you."

Dad, still sitting on the bench, grabbed Mom's wrist, but she shook him off.

"I know you're curious about him," Mom said to me. "I get that. But please don't be mad at me. None of this is my fault. Marcus being in prison is not my fault."

Out of the corner of my eye, I noticed a few people staring at us. I ignored them.

"It's your fault I can't write to him," I said. "My own father! You're keeping him from me!"

"Yes. And I'm doing the right thing," Mom said.

I stared at her, my eyes filling with tears, as she stood there breathing heavily. I turned away from her, and then felt something cold and wet on my fingers. My ice cream cone was dripping everywhere. I walked to the nearest trash can and threw the cone into it. Dad came up behind me and handed me a couple of napkins, which I used to wipe my hands off. He tried to put his arm around me, but I wiggled out of his way.

"Let's go home," Dad said quietly.

Without a word, I followed him back to where we parked the car. Mom trailed behind us.

On the drive back, part of me wished I hadn't ruined the night by bringing up Marcus at all. But most of me was determined to prove them wrong.

Chapter Nineteen

The Ari's Cakes kitchen was really quiet when I walked in the next morning. Vincent, wearing a red bandanna, was overseeing the mixer, and Rosa was setting the timer on the wall of ovens. Liz was at the big metal table in the middle of the room, using a piping bag to pipe shimmery dark-blue icing onto what looked like vanilla cupcakes. Corey, on the other side of the table, carefully placed fondant decorations on the iced cupcakes. The finished ones each had a small, silver crescent moon and three mini gold stars. Ariana was helping Liz with the icing, and I watched in amazement as she piped a whole row super fast.

Everyone was so focused on what they were working on that nobody noticed me walk into the kitchen. I went up to Ariana and cleared my throat. "Um, good morning."

"Oh—morning, Zoe," Ariana said as she continued piping.

"What's going on?" I asked.

"We have a huge rush order this morning. Five hundred decorated cupcakes need to be ready by noon. It's all hands on deck."

"Cool! What should I do?" I asked.

Ariana paused her icing just long enough to glance at everyone else around the kitchen. "Why don't you help Corey with the fondant. He's cutting out moons and stars, so super simple, but there are a million of them."

"Okay."

I walked around the table until I was next to Corey.

"Hi, Corey," I said. "How can I help?"

"Hey, Zoe. Let's see. Can you roll out more fondant?" He pointed to two huge balls of fondant—one was gold, and the other was silver. "You can start with the gold. Take that rolling pin, and roll it out like dough. Sprinkle some confectioners' sugar on the table first. It should be about half an inch all around when you're done."

"Got it." It sounded easy enough. I picked up the rolling pin and got to work. It took some strength at first to get the huge ball to flatten out, but then it was just a matter of rolling it over and over until it was flat enough.

As I rolled, my mind wandered back to my fight with Mom outside of J.P. Licks. I hadn't been able to think about much else all morning. She was never going to take my side—not unless I found Marcus's alibi witness and showed her that he really was innocent. If he truly *was* innocent . . . I didn't want Mom to be right about him.

What I really wanted to do was bang on the fondant over and over with the rolling pin until all my anger at Mom came out of me. But of course, I couldn't do that— not unless I wanted Ariana to kick me out of her kitchen.

I rolled and rolled, and daydreamed about finding Marcus's witness and being able to tell Mom that she was wrong. She'd have to apologize, and the Innocence Project would get Marcus out of prison. I'd finally get to meet him. We could play basketball together, or go to a Celtics game. He could cook me dinner, and I'd bake the dessert. Maybe I'd even have my own cookbook, because Mom and Dad would let me go on the *Kids Bake Challenge!*, and of course I'd win. And Marcus could be there to see it.

"Not so hard, Zoe," Ariana said, suddenly beside me.

"Huh?" I looked down at the fondant. *Shoot.* I must've pushed too hard on the rolling pin, and now the fondant was way too thin. "Sorry! I'll start over." I started to pick up the fondant so I could shape it back into another ball.

Ariana looked at the clock on the wall and then back at me. "You know what, I'll take over. Why don't you go up front, see if Gabe needs any help with customers."

"Wait. I can fix it."

"I know. It's just, this is for a really important customer, and I'd rather take care of it myself." She patted my shoulder. "I bet Gabe could use some help."

"Okay . . . ," I said reluctantly. I watched for a few seconds while Ariana started piling the fondant back up until it looked like a mound of clay again.

It suddenly felt like a mound of clay was sitting in my gut.

I left the kitchen and found Gabe up front, ringing up a customer. When he was finished, I said, "Ariana says you need help up here?"

"Oh, really?" Gabe said, looking around the shop. "Hmm. We're kinda slow today. But I know what you can help with. One sec." He left and went into the kitchen.

Maybe I'd get to help with the window display. That could be super fun.

But then Gabe came back with a box. A box that looked really familiar.

No . . .

He put it on the floor and opened it. Sure enough, it was filled with flat cardboard in the shop's signature blue. Gabe opened a cabinet under the coffee machine. "We're short on boxes under here. Think you can help me put some together? It's super easy."

"Oh, I know." I picked up a box and quickly assembled it.

"That's perfect!" he said, as if it was actually hard to do.

"And when you're done, you can help me refill the napkin holders."

Great. I forced a smile, and got to work.

Back to boxes, and it was all my fault for getting distracted in the kitchen.

I couldn't let that happen again. I wouldn't. *What would Ruby Willow do?* She'd put all of her energy into accomplishing her goal, just like when she was on *Kids Bake Challenge!* If I was going to make it onto that show, if I was going to be a real pastry chef one day, I had to focus on baking.

There was only one month left of summer and my internship, and I'd been so absorbed in thinking about Marcus that I hadn't even come up with my own cupcake recipe yet.

I had to get to work—and fast.

I brainstormed cupcake ideas over the next couple of days, but it was even harder than I thought. My list included lemonade cupcakes—inspired by Grandma's tea—and a sweet and savory cupcake that included potato chips. But none of those seemed original enough.

When Grandma showed up with Marcus's next letter, I opened it right away, happy for the distraction.

To my Little Tomato,

Wow. Wow, wow, wow. That is what went through my head when I opened your letter and saw your school photo. You are such a beautiful girl. You definitely have your mom's smile. Thank you so much for sharing it with me. I will cherish it forever.

You asked for a recipe. My mom makes the best macaroni and cheese. Just thinking about it makes my mouth water. I know that recipe by heart, so I wrote it on the back of this letter. If you make it, I'd love to know what you think.

Life in here is nothing like my life before, but I still get to read books, exercise, and watch TV. Sometimes I'll join a pickup game of basketball in the rec yard. I have a couple friends—guys that have been here a while like me, and aren't trying to get into trouble.

I know my last letter was probably confusing. I wish we lived in a fairer world, where only guilty people went to prison. But I think the best thing for us to do is leave the past behind us, as I've tried to do, and focus on the here and now. Right now, I'm happy that I got your letter and this beautiful picture.

I've been thinking. Your grandma said I could call you at her house. Maybe we should try that. How about on August 15 around three p.m.? By then, you should have this letter and can hopefully make plans to be at your grandma's house.

In terms of a unique ingredient for a cupcake, that's hard! But you know, when I was younger my favorite thing to eat was cereal. It's so bad, but my favorite was always the colorful sugary cereals. I rotated between all of them. I'd find the biggest bowl in our kitchen and fill it up. The cereal would turn the milk different colors, and I'd sit on the couch with the humongous bowl on my lap, watching

150

cartoons. Maybe you can make some kind of cereal cupcake?

Finally, here's a new song for your playlist: "Golden," by Jill Scott.

Love,

Marcus

Chapter Twenty

Trevor's eyes widened as he watched me take the boxes out of the grocery bag and line them up on his kitchen counter. Froot Loops. Reese's Puffs. Cinnamon Toast Crunch. Cocoa Pebbles.

"What's with all the cereal?" Trevor asked.

"I'm gonna use one of them in a cupcake recipe." Cereal cupcakes! It was such a good idea; I wished I'd thought of it myself. Everyone loved cereal, especially the sugary kind. I couldn't wait to start experimenting, so after I got Marcus's letter, I asked Grandma to take me to the grocery store again. She wouldn't let me get full boxes of each cereal, but she got me a variety pack of the mini boxes when I told her why I needed them.

"Cereal cupcakes?" Trevor asked, scratching his nose.

"Yes. Wait, does that not sound good?"

"No. I mean, I don't know."

"I think it could be really yummy," I said. "But first I have to figure out which cereal to use. Wanna help me taste-test them?"

Trevor's eyes lit up. "Sure! Mom never lets me eat this stuff. She says there's too much sugar."

"That's kind of the point of it," I said.

He grabbed two bowls from the cabinet, two spoons from the drawer, and the carton of milk from the refrigerator.

Trevor went straight for the Cocoa Pebbles, filling his bowl and pouring milk on top. "Mmm," he said as he chewed his first bite. "I vote for these."

"You're only voting for those because they're chocolate."

"And?"

I shrugged and poured myself a small bowl of it, too. It was pretty chocolaty, but I could imagine pairing it with peanut butter. Like, maybe a chocolate peanut butter cupcake with Cocoa Pebbles in the batter, so when you bit into the finished cupcake, you'd get crunchy bits. And then I could put more of the flakes in vanilla buttercream icing.

I poured the rest of the cereal in the trash so I could try the next one.

"What are you doing?" Trevor's face twisted in offense. "You're wasting perfectly good cereal!"

I rolled my eyes at him and grabbed the next box— Froot Loops. "I like the idea of using this one," I told Trevor. "Because it's so colorful. Maybe I could make tie-dye cupcakes or something." I took a bite and grimaced. It was a little too sweet, like in a fake way. "Hmm." I stared at the bowl and thought about how I could make it work.

Then there was the sound of footsteps on our front porch, and a knock at Trevor's front door.

"Trev! You home?" someone called out.

I froze. That was Lincoln's voice. He was probably with Sean.

Trevor glanced at me and then toward the front of his house.

"One sec," he said to me. "I'll . . . tell them I'm busy."

I didn't say anything as Trevor left the room. Once he went down the hall to open the front door, I moved into the hallway and stood to the side of the staircase. I didn't dare move closer to the front door, because I didn't want the boys to see me. This meant I couldn't see them either, but I could hear every word.

This better not be a repeat of what happened the last time I listened in.

"You free to play?" Sean asked once Trevor opened the door. There was the sound of a basketball dribbling on the porch.

"Can't today," Trevor said.

"Why not?"

I held my breath.

"I'm doing something." He paused. "Zoe's over."

"Washington?" Lincoln said. "Why are you hanging out with *her*?"

"Did your parents make you?" Sean asked. "That really sucks."

"Just ditch her," Lincoln said.

"No," Trevor said. "My parents didn't make me. We're . . ."

I squeezed my hands together.

". . . She's my friend."

Lincoln and Sean broke out laughing, but then they trailed off.

"Wait, you're serious?" Lincoln asked.

"Yeah," Trevor said. "She's cool. I never should've said that stuff about her. I didn't mean it."

155

"Ohh, I get it," Sean said. "She's your girlfriend now."

Lincoln burst out laughing.

My face got really hot, and I buried it in my hands.

"What? No," Trevor said. "It's not like that."

"You totally like her!" Lincoln said.

"No!" Trevor said.

I looked up at the wall. *Should I run back to the kitchen? Will they hear me if I do?*

"I like her as a friend," Trevor said. "You guys have to shut up about her. Okay?"

"Okaaay," Sean said.

"Yeah, whatever," Lincoln said. "So you can't hang out?"

"I'll catch up with you later," Trevor said.

"Later," Lincoln and Sean said at the same time.

Trevor's storm door creaked open and shut, and I turned around and jetted back into the kitchen. I picked up a box of cereal and pretended to focus on reading it.

A couple of seconds later, Trevor walked in. "So you heard that."

"Heard what?"

"I saw you run back into the kitchen when I came inside."

"Oh," I said.

"I'm sorry they're such jerks," Trevor said.

I didn't know what to say, so I picked up my cereal bowl from before and took a bite of the Froot Loops. They'd turned totally soggy. Gross. But then I dipped my spoon back into the milk, to wash down the soggy cereal. By itself, the milk was actually pretty yummy. The cereal sweetened it up, so it wasn't as sweet as the cereal itself, but almost. I took another sip, and the wheels in my brain started turning.

I smiled at Trevor. "I think I know what cupcakes I'm gonna bake."

I wouldn't just make cereal cupcakes. I'd make cereal milk cupcakes. I'd made vanilla cupcakes so many times; I had that recipe memorized already. All I'd have to do was swap out the regular milk for the Froot Loops–flavored milk. Then I could use food coloring to make the cupcakes tie-dye to match the cereal. Last, I could crumble some of the Froot Loops on top of the vanilla icing, for some extra pizazz.

After dinner a few days later, Mom and Dad were cuddled together on the couch, watching some documentary. I wished I could start baking without having to tell them first, but I didn't want to get in trouble. I stood in the doorway and asked, "Can I use the oven?"

They both glanced up from the television. "What are you baking?" Dad asked.

"Cupcakes."

"As long as you save one for me," Dad said. "And don't forget to use the oven mitts."

"Thanks." I ran back to the kitchen before one of them could offer to be my sous-chef.

First, I had to make the cereal milk. I poured one and a half cups of milk into a stainless-steel mixing bowl and added Froot Loops to it. I wasn't sure how much to add, or how long the cereal would have to sit in the milk to flavor it. At Trevor's house, it'd only been around ten minutes, so I tried that.

Then I turned the oven on to preheat to 350 degrees and started on my vanilla cupcake recipe. This was my favorite part, because I got to use my stand mixer, which I'd gotten for Christmas the previous year. It was yellow, the color of butter and sunshine. Looking at it made me happy.

I added the sugar, flour, baking powder, and salt to the mixer and turned it on. Once it was all mixed up, I started combining the wet ingredients into a separate bowl. When it was time to add milk, I dipped a clean spoon into the Froot Loops milk and tasted it. It could taste a little stronger, so I left it for another ten minutes before I added the cereal milk to my cupcake batter.

I decided not to bother with the food coloring this time. I wanted to make sure I got the recipe right first.

Once everything was all mixed up, I scooped the batter into my cupcake pan and put it in the oven, setting the timer for twenty minutes.

While I waited, I started thinking about talking on the phone with Marcus. I wondered what he'd sound like. Would he have a really deep voice? Would he sound nice, or scary?

I had to make sure I asked Marcus for his alibi witness's name, since he didn't give it to me in his last letter. He may have wanted to leave the past behind him, but I was only getting started. When he heard how much it meant to me, he'd have to give me the name.

When the timer went off, I stuck toothpicks into a couple of the cupcakes to make sure they were done. The toothpicks came out a bit wet, so I added two more minutes to the timer and put them back in the oven.

When they were finally done, I took them out to let them cool. And then I grabbed a cupcake and broke off a piece.

Please taste good.

I took a bite, and then almost spit it out. Way too sweet! Guess the extra sugar in the milk was too much. I'd probably have to add less sugar to the next batch to even it out. Maybe I could ask Ariana or Vincent for their advice. No—I wanted to figure this out on my own. I could do what Ariana did—bake a couple of small batches with different amounts of sugar, so I could see which one tasted the best.

On the plus side, the cupcake did sort of taste like Froot Loops. My recipe was on the right track, and I wouldn't stop trying until I nailed it.

I put the leftover cupcakes in a Tupperware container so Dad could bring them to work the next day. He once told me that his coworkers would eat any treats that he put in the office pantry.

My parents kept a notebook next to the fridge to write down whatever groceries we needed for the week. I added sugar and flour to the list, since I was running low. Then I remembered Marcus's macaroni and cheese recipe. I didn't really know how to cook, but his recipe hadn't seemed too hard. I bet I could make it. I ran into my room and snapped a picture of the recipe on the back of his last letter before hiding it again.

Mom was refilling her water cup when I got back to the kitchen. Things were still tense between us since our fight outside of J.P. Licks, so I ignored her. But I could sense her watching me as I added the macaroni and cheese ingredients to the grocery list and put the notepad back in its spot.

She picked it up and wrote something on it. "Are you going to bake something with cheese in it?" she asked.

"No," I said. "I want to make macaroni and cheese from scratch."

"Really?"

"Yeah. Um, with Grandma. We're going to do it together." That hadn't been my plan, but it actually would be nice to make it with her. I could even tell her that it was Marcus's recipe.

Mom nodded. "That sounds nice. Make sure you save some for Dad and me to try."

She didn't deserve Marcus's macaroni and cheese. Not when she was keeping him from me.

Chapter Twenty-One

Marcus's call was scheduled for Monday afternoon, so it was all I could think about while at Ari's Cakes. Even though I got to bake with Vincent again, I couldn't wait for the morning to be over.

Grandma took me straight to her house after picking me up. She made me lunch, but I could barely eat.

At 2:55 p.m., I got Grandma's cordless phone and sat it on the coffee table. I stared at it, my knees bouncing. Finally, at 3:07, the phone rang.

I grabbed the phone as it rang a second time. My stomach flip-flopped.

Grandma rushed into the living room. "Do you want to answer it?" she asked.

I nodded. There was no time for me to build up the courage. The phone would only ring so many times. I pressed the Call button. ". . . Hello?" My voice was as small as a mouse.

The millisecond that passed while I waited for Marcus to come on the line felt like a million years. I held my breath.

But I didn't hear Marcus. Instead, a recording came on the line, saying, "This is a collect call from an inmate at the Massachusetts State Penitentiary . . . ," before another person chimed in.

"Marcus Johnson." *Marcus's voice.* My eyes widened as Grandma stood there watching me.

The other voice returned and said the call would be recorded and monitored, and to press 1 if I wanted to proceed. I could barely pay attention. I held on to the phone tighter so I wouldn't drop it.

"It's h-him," I stuttered. "It says I have to press 1.'" But I could barely move. *If I pull the phone away from my ear, I might miss something,* I thought. I should've put it on speaker right after I answered. But it was too late now—I might end up hanging up by mistake. I quickly pulled the phone away from my face and stared at the numbers. Then my brain went blank.

"Let me." Grandma took the phone, pressed 1, and put it to her own ear.

"Marcus? Hi, it's Jeanette." She stopped talking and I could hear a murmur come through the phone—Marcus's voice. I couldn't believe I was about to talk to him.

"I'm doing well, thank you." There was a pause, and more murmuring. "Yes, she's right here. Hold on." Grandma rested the phone on her shoulder and spoke softly. "Do you still want to talk to him?"

I nodded.

"You sure? It's okay if you changed your mind."

"I'm sure," I said. "I'm just nervous."

Grandma gave me a warm smile. "Of course you are, but it's only a phone call. I'll be right here. If you don't want to talk anymore, hand the phone back to me, and I'll take care of it. Okay?"

I took a deep breath. Grandma was right—it was only a phone call. What was the worst that could happen? Except, I could think of a bunch of things. What if Marcus didn't sound as nice on the phone as he did in his letters? What if he said something scary to me? Or I heard something scary happening in the prison in the background? I had no idea what prison was like.

But I had to at least try. "All right."

Grandma put the phone back to her ear. "Okay, here's Zoe."

She handed the phone to me and I slowly put it to my ear. "Hello?" I said, tentative and low.

"My Little Tomato," Marcus said, and he made a sort of laugh, like he also couldn't believe we were actually talking. "Zoe. I'm so happy to hear your voice."

His voice was deep, but not in a scary way. More in a comforting way, like Morgan Freeman's voice when he narrated animated movies.

Tears sprang into my eyes. Even though I couldn't see Marcus on the other end of the line, I could tell that he might be crying too. He exhaled loudly into the phone, and his breath sounded uneven.

I tried to imagine him in his orange jumpsuit, holding the phone. There was noise in the background, though I couldn't make it out exactly, so he must've been in a room with other convicts.

"Me too." I wasn't sure what else to say. I wanted to hear Marcus talk some more.

"How are you?" he asked.

"I'm okay. How are you?"

"Really good now that I'm talking to you. You're making my day. No, my month."

I smiled, and Grandma gave me a look as if to say, "Everything good?" I nodded at her, and Grandma smiled back.

"I've been listening to the Little Tomato playlist a lot," I told him. "The Jill Scott song has been stuck in my head for the last couple of days."

"That's great," Marcus said.

"I'm going to make your macaroni and cheese recipe," I told him. "Thanks for sharing it."

"I know you'll do a good job making it," he said.

"It's too bad I can't send you some in the mail," I said. Marcus laughed.

"I wish you could send me a picture of you," I said. "I have one from when you were in high school, but I want to know what you look like now."

"You have a picture of me?" Marcus asked. "Which one?"

"It's you at a Celtics game, wearing one of their sweatshirts."

Marcus laughed again. "I know exactly which picture you're talking about. Your mom used to have it in a frame. She gave me the tickets as a surprise for my birthday. The Celtics won, too. It was amazing."

It was hard to imagine Mom being happy with Marcus, knowing how she felt about him now.

We were silent for a moment, and I wondered if Marcus was thinking about Mom.

"Well, anyway," Marcus said. "I don't think I look that different now—just older. Bigger. I was kind of scrawny back then. And I have to shave more now."

In my mind, I tried to replace the image of Marcus that I knew with the one he described. I wished I could see him in real life.

I was about to ask him if he got to watch any basketball in prison, but then I heard shouting in the background.

"Time to get off," someone yelled.

"What was that?" I asked, suddenly feeling scared for Marcus. If he was innocent, then he was surrounded by criminals. Unless there were other innocent people in his prison with him. It was still hard to wrap my head around it.

"Zoe, I have to go." Marcus sounded rushed all of a sudden—and sad. "I'm really sorry, but it's time for me to get off the phone."

"You can't go yet," I said. "We only started talking."

Then I remembered. I didn't ask him about his alibi witness! I didn't want to wait to ask him in another letter. I needed more time on our call.

"I'm sorry. Those are the rules. We'll talk again, I promise," he said.

"Wait. Can you call me again tomorrow, same time? *Please?*" I said the words as fast as I could.

"Okay, I'll try my best. Goodbye, my Little Tomato."

"Okay. Bye," I said, but Marcus was already gone. There was a click as the call ended.

I put the phone down on the coffee table and looked up at Grandma.

"He said he might call me again tomorrow," I said, the words rushing from my mouth. "I hope that's okay. I needed more time."

Grandma nodded, her smile warm. "That's fine."

I hoped nothing prevented Marcus from calling me back.

Chapter Twenty-Two

To help pass the time while I waited for Marcus's second call the next day, I brought my macaroni and cheese ingredients to Grandma's house so we could make Marcus's recipe together for lunch.

"I have no idea what I'm doing," I told Grandma. "I'm only good with sweet stuff."

Grandma smiled. "That's why there's a recipe. You follow steps just like with baking. Here, let me see it."

I handed her Marcus's letter, which had the recipe on the back.

"Why don't you start grating the cheese?" Grandma

asked. "I'll put a pot of water on to boil and preheat the oven."

"Okay."

Grandma took out a cheese grater and I got to work on the huge block of mild cheddar cheese. After that I grated the sharp cheddar and Monterey Jack cheeses. By the time I was done with all that grating, my right arm felt like rubber.

The next steps were easy. As the pasta cooked, Grandma and I made the cheese sauce by adding the grated cheeses to milk and heavy cream in a pot. We added some seasonings, like salt, pepper, and paprika, and mixed it all together.

"Let's taste the sauce to make sure the seasonings are right," Grandma told me.

We dipped spoons into the mixture and tasted it.

"What do you think?" Grandma asked.

"Maybe more paprika?" I said. "I'm not sure I taste a lot of spice." What I tasted was a whole lot of cheese.

"Sounds good to me," Grandma said, and I shook a little more paprika into the mixture.

Marcus's recipe said to add a couple of eggs next, so we did that.

When the timer went off for the pasta, I went for the colander, but Grandma stopped me.

"You should always taste the pasta first, to make sure it's ready." She used a spoon to scoop a few macaroni noodles out of the pot. She blew on them, and then popped one in her mouth and handed me the other. It tasted pretty good to me.

"Perfectly al dente," Grandma said.

"Al *what*-te?" I asked.

She laughed. "It's a term chefs use to describe the texture of the pasta. You want it to still be a little firm when you bite into it."

"Oh."

We drained the macaroni and then poured it into a baking dish. We poured the cheese sauce on top and mixed it all together. I loved the weird squishy sound the macaroni made as we mixed the cheese in. Finally, we sprinkled some more shredded cheese on top and put the baking dish in the oven.

I helped Grandma clean up the mess while the mac and cheese baked.

"Are you excited to talk to Marcus again?" she asked as she opened her dishwasher.

"Yes. And nervous," I said. "But mostly excited. It was really nice to get to hear his voice. Thank you for letting me."

Grandma smiled. "You're welcome, baby."

When the timer went off, we took the macaroni and cheese out of the oven. The layer of cheese on the top was a toasty brown color, and more cheese bubbled underneath. It smelled amazing. I took a picture of the dish with my phone. I actually cooked something!

Grandma scooped some onto plates for us, with salad on the side.

"This is delicious," Grandma said after she took her first bite. "You did a great job."

It *was* really good. I couldn't wait to tell Marcus.

When it got close to the time that Marcus would call, I went into Grandma's living room, grabbed the phone, and practiced pressing the 1 button. I had my journal next to me so I could write down everything Marcus told me about his alibi witness.

When the phone rang at 3:25, I startled again. It was just like the day before. Grandma rushed into the living room with her mug of tea. I picked up the phone and there was the recorded voice again, saying it was a collect call from Marcus Johnson. I beamed, this time pressing 1 without any trouble.

"Hello?" Marcus asked.

"Hi." I exhaled into the phone. "It's Zoe."

"My Little Tomato," he said, and I could tell he was smiling again. "I'm sorry we got cut off yesterday like that."

"That's okay. I'm glad we get to talk again." Then I said, "Guess what I made today?"

"What?" Marcus asked.

"Your mac and cheese recipe! Grandma and I had it for lunch. It tasted really good."

"That's great!" Marcus said, laughing. "I wish I could taste it."

"Me too."

"What else is going on?" Marcus asked.

"Well, I wanted to ask you something." I took a deep breath. "I know you said you don't want to talk about the past and whatever, but I want to talk to your alibi witness, and hear her side of the story. Can you tell me her name?"

"I'm sorry, but I can't do that," Marcus said. "I don't want you getting involved in this."

"If it's true that you're innocent, I want to know," I said.

There was silence on the line.

"Sweetheart," Marcus said, now sounding sad.

"No," I said. "Please don't say that like I'm a little kid who can't handle things. I'm old enough to understand this. In case you forgot, I'm twelve years old."

Marcus sighed. "You're a smart kid, I know that. But this stuff is complicated."

"I know that people go to jail even when they don't deserve to," I said. "I didn't used to know that, but I do now. Also, I read all about the Innocence Project. Have you heard of them?"

"I have, but—"

"Maybe they can help you," I said.

"Zoe . . ."

I didn't want to waste any more time. I needed Marcus to let me do this. But how would I convince him to give me the name? "How am I supposed to know that you're really innocent?" I made my voice serious. "I barely know anything about you. You could be lying to me."

"I told you I wouldn't lie to you," Marcus said.

"But how do I know you aren't lying about that?"

He breathed into the phone. "You don't. I guess you have to decide if you trust me. I hope you do."

"Well," I said, "I want to know for sure if you're innocent. If you don't tell me who the witness is, then it must be because you made her up. Because you really did kill someone." My voice cracked. What if he really did make the alibi witness up?

"I didn't ki—" Marcus started to say, but then stopped. "I didn't do it."

"Then why aren't you fighting harder to get out of prison?" I asked. My heart began to race. What if I couldn't convince Marcus to give me the name? I wouldn't be able to figure out the truth, or get the chance to ever be with him.

"So you can see me," I added after a breath. "So you can be my dad."

"Oh, Zoe," Marcus said. "I love you so much, you know that? I would do anything—" His voice broke, and he paused. "I would give anything to be there with you, to be your dad.

"And I want you to know that I did fight," Marcus continued. "I fought really hard my first few years here. I filed for an appeal and everything. But it didn't work. The court still thinks I'm guilty. I can't go through that again. I decided a while ago to accept my fate and try to make the best of it in here. In another thirteen years, I'll be eligible for parole. I'm holding on to hope that I'll get out then."

I'd be twenty-five years old in thirteen years. Even if he could get out of prison then, that was a very long time from now—especially if he was innocent. I couldn't wait that long. I wanted to fight for him.

"Please," I begged. "If you really love me, if you'd really do anything, then this is the one thing I'm asking for. Please just tell me her name. I need to know."

Marcus sighed heavily into the phone, and then there was silence for a few moments. For a second, I thought the call had gotten disconnected.

But then Marcus finally said, "Okay. Her name is Susan Thomas."

I exhaled with relief and wrote down the name Susan Thomas in big, bold letters in my journal. Then I underlined it a couple of times. "Grandma said you met her at a tag sale."

"Right. The day before it happened, I saw her ad on Craigslist. She was getting rid of a bunch of stuff at her house in Brookline and I wanted to check out her futon. I called her and we set up a time to meet the next day—the day Lucy was killed.

"The problem is," Marcus continued, "she was about to move. That was why she was getting rid of stuff. I don't know where she was moving, but I don't think she's at the old address anymore."

If I looked her up, I could probably find her new address. "What do you remember about her?" I asked. "How old was she? What did she look like?"

"She was white with straight brown hair and brown eyes. She had freckles on her face, that part I remember. I don't know how old she was, maybe in her early thirties."

I wrote everything down. I racked my brain and tried to think of what else I would need to know. "Anything else? Do you know what her job was?" If I couldn't find out where she lived, I might be able to track her down through her job, if she was still there. Or even if she moved.

"She mentioned students at one point," Marcus said. "I don't know for sure, but she might've been a teacher. We talked for a few minutes when I went to check out the futon. I know she was married, and didn't have any kids at that time. But I didn't really learn much else about her. I was there to buy stuff from her. And when I told my lawyer about her, he said he'd look into it, but then he never found her. That's all I remember, Zoe."

"Okay," I said. It wasn't much, but it was a start. "Thank you for telling me."

"I really don't want you getting involved with this," Marcus said. "Please, just live your life and be happy, okay? That's what I really want for you."

"I will," I said. *After I find your witness.*

We talked for a few more minutes, and I asked him if he ever got to watch basketball in prison.

"Sometimes," he said. "When I'm lucky."

A few more minutes after that, he had to go. I didn't know when we'd get to talk on the phone again, but we agreed to keep writing letters.

When I got off the phone, I stared at all of the notes I took in my journal. *Susan Thomas, wherever you are, I'm going to find you.*

Chapter Twenty-Three

"What was that all about?" Grandma asked.

"What?" I looked up from my journal.

"You told Marcus you were going to look for his alibi witness?"

"Oh. Yes." I had no idea where Susan Thomas lived, but I figured I could track her down online first, and then figure out how to get to her later.

Grandma frowned. "That's not a good idea."

"What do you mean?" I asked. "You said yourself that you think he's innocent. I want to know for sure."

"But you can't go looking for a stranger."

"Why not?"

Grandma narrowed her eyes at me. "You know why not. It could be dangerous." Then she said, "You know, I've been thinking that it's time to tell your parents what we've been up to. It's not good that we've been lying to them for this long."

Panic shot up my spine. "You can't!"

If Grandma told my parents now, the letters would end, and I'd definitely get in trouble for lying. I wouldn't be able to keep getting to know Marcus, and I'd never find out whether he really was innocent. I couldn't let either of those things happen.

How could I get Grandma to change her mind?

"Please," I told her. "I promise I'll forget about the alibi witness, okay? But please let me keep writing to Marcus. Mom won't let me if she finds out, I know it. And then that'll be it."

I watched as Grandma considered this for the longest ten seconds of my life.

Clasping her hands together, she finally said, "Fine. You can keep writing to him. But no more talk about this alibi witness, okay? And we have to come clean to your parents at some point soon."

Phew, I thought, but I kept a straight face. "Okay."

"Good." She smiled. "Want some tea? I still have some of that pink lemonade one."

"Sure," I said, and Grandma left me in her living room.

There was no way I could forget about Marcus's alibi witness, especially now that I had her name. If Grandma wasn't going to help me, I'd have to find her on my own, without anyone finding out.

There was an icky feeling in the pit of my stomach when I thought about lying to Grandma, the one person who'd helped me keep writing to Marcus—even talk to him on the phone. But I had to find Susan Thomas. I had to.

All of the lying was wrong, I knew that. But maybe it was okay to do something wrong if you were doing it for the right reason.

I didn't know how much time I had, how long Grandma would wait before finally telling my parents about my communication with Marcus. All I knew was that I needed to find Susan Thomas fast.

And then I remembered. I wouldn't have to do this on my own after all.

I picked up my phone and texted Trevor.

Susan Thomas. It was such a simple name, and also a pretty popular one. When I typed it into the search browser, over 150 million results popped up. There were photos of girls and women of all different ages, professional websites, personal blogs, social media pages, and more. When I skimmed through some of the sites, I saw that they were all over the country, and some even lived abroad. Lots of them had brown hair and brown eyes, and many of those Susan Thomases had freckles.

When I changed my search to "Susan Thomas Brookline MA," the results went down to one million. Which was better, but not good enough.

I was over at Trevor's house so we could search together. When I'd texted him to ask for his help, he immediately agreed. It was both weird and super familiar to be back in Trevor's room, which was really neat, as always. His bed was made, and there was a new basketball poster above his desk, plus even more novels on his bookshelf. We sat next to each other at his desk in front of his computer.

"I might never find her." I frowned at the computer screen. How would I narrow down all of these results to the one Susan Thomas I needed to find?

"We just started looking," Trevor said. "We'll find her, even if we have to message every single Susan Thomas."

"That could take forever."

Trevor shrugged. "My dad's always telling me I have all the time in the world to do things."

"But if Marcus is innocent, he doesn't have all the time in the world," I said. "I hate thinking of him in there,

181

surrounded by criminals, if he's really innocent. He said he has friends there, and not everybody in jail is bad, but I think he was only saying that to make me feel better."

"Did Marcus say that he remembered anything else?"

I glanced at my journal again. Underneath Susan's name and physical description, I'd written "students." "Right! Marcus said he thought she was a teacher, because she said the word 'students' when they talked."

Trevor pulled the keyboard closer. In the search box, he typed in, "Susan Thomas Brookline MA teacher." Within the top results was the website for Brookline Elementary School.

"Click on that," I told him.

When he did, a page popped up showing the staff at the school. In the middle of the page was a picture of a Susan Thomas, who was a second-grade teacher. She had brown hair, though it was pretty light, almost blond. Her eyes were definitely brown, though. I couldn't spot any freckles, but it looked like she was wearing makeup, so maybe she'd covered them up. Marcus had said she was in her thirties back then, so she was probably in her forties now. I couldn't really tell how old this woman was.

"Maybe that's her," I said. "What do you think?"

Trevor shrugged. "She's a teacher in Brookline, and she pretty much fits the description."

"Okay!" I smiled. "But wait. Marcus said she was moving. Why do you think she's still living in Brookline, then?"

"Maybe she just moved to a different house in Brookline," Trevor said.

I nodded. "That makes sense. This was super easy."

"We had good clues."

I nodded, but part of me wondered if it'd been *too* easy. If Susan Thomas was this easy to find, why didn't Marcus's lawyer bother to look for her? Grandma's theory that he didn't care what happened to Marcus seemed even more likely.

Susan's email was listed on the school's website, next to her bio.

"I guess I'll send her an email, and see if she remembers Marcus," I said.

"Good idea," Trevor said.

I opened up my email in a new browser window and started typing.

From: Zoe Washington
To: Susan Thomas
Subject: Do you know Marcus Johnson?

Dear Ms. Thomas,

    I'm looking for someone with your name, who met

my dad. It was 13 years ago, and he came to your house in Brookline to buy some stuff at your tag sale. Could that be you?

I attached his picture. Do you recognize him? I really hope you do.

This is really important, so please write back soon.

Sincerely,

Zoe Washington

Marcus's picture was tucked inside my journal, so I took it out and snapped a photo of it with my phone. It was taken when he was still in high school, so a couple of years before the crime happened, but I thought that it was better than showing Ms. Thomas his mug shot or pictures from the trial. I didn't want her to see him that way and get it in her head that he was guilty.

I emailed the picture to myself so I could open it on Trevor's computer. Then I attached it to the email to Susan, read it one more time, and clicked Send.

I leaned back into my seat and looked at Trevor. "What do we do now?"

He shrugged. "I guess we wait to hear back from her."

I'd already waited twelve years to speak to Marcus. How much longer would I have to wait for the truth?

Chapter Twenty-Four

I started checking my inbox constantly for an email to come in. I even put a special notification ringtone on my phone that sounded like birds chirping. Trevor and I also searched for other Susan Thomases who could've possibly met Marcus, but the only other person who seemed like she could be a match now lived all the way in California. I sent her an email too, just in case. She got back to me right away, saying that she never had a garage sale when she lived in Brookline. So it *had* to be the teacher we'd found.

The only thing that kept me distracted from my inbox was baking. I spent all of Thursday afternoon working on my cereal cupcake recipe.

I decided to do what I'd learned at Ari's Cakes—make a few small batches of cupcake batter, each with different amounts of sugar. I also wanted to experiment with the amount of cereal flavor in the milk, so I let the cereal sit in some of the milk longer.

We only had one stand mixer in our kitchen and two mixing bowls for it. I made my first batch, and then scooped the batter into one row of my cupcake pan, using blue painter's tape I found in the junk drawer to label which recipe it was. When I was done, I made my second batch, adjusting the ingredients a little. I had to clean the mixing bowls before I could make the next two batches. The whole process took even longer because I kept stopping to check my phone in between steps, to make sure my ringtone notification was still on and the volume was still up.

When all the batches were done and my cupcake pan was full of the different recipes, I put them in the oven to bake.

I leaned against the counter and checked my phone. Then I checked the oven timer. Then I went back to my phone.

Ugh, I needed to do something else.

I decided to get a head start on cleaning my baking mess, something I usually left until after my treats were out of the oven, cooling. I put all of my ingredients away, wiped down the countertops, mopped up the flour that had fallen on the floor, and cleaned all the bowls and utensils I'd used. Butternut came into the room, so I gave him a few treats.

Finally, the timer went off, and I took the cupcakes out of the oven. I let them cool for a few minutes, then started tasting them one recipe at a time.

There was a clear winner. The ones with less sugar and more-saturated cereal milk. It tasted delicious! It had the essence of the Froot Loops, without being too sweet.

I'd done it. I'd created my own cupcake recipe! I did a happy dance around the kitchen island, but froze when I heard my phone chirp.

An email. I opened up the notification on my phone. It wasn't from Susan Thomas.

It was from Anthony Miller, Marcus's lawyer. I'd started to think I'd never hear from him.

The email was only a couple of sentences. Mr. Miller apologized for taking so long to respond, but then gave his phone number and said I could call him with my questions about Marcus's case.

I immediately called Mr. Miller's office. My heart pounded as the phone rang.

Finally, it picked up. "Anthony Miller's office," a voice on the other line said.

"Hi, um, may I speak to Mr. Miller?" I asked.

"May I ask who's calling?" the woman asked.

"Zoe Washington. I'm returning his call," I lied.

"One moment please," she said.

A minute later, a man's voice got on the line. "This is Anthony Miller."

"Oh, hi, Mr. Miller. I'm Zoe. Zoe Washington. I wrote to you asking about Marcus Johnson's case, and you said I could call you with questions." By the end of that sentence, I was sweating.

"Right . . . ," Mr. Miller said, sounding skeptical. It made me second-guess myself for a moment. Had I called the right person?

"You're the one who sent the email?" Mr. Miller asked. "How old are you?"

"I'm twelve." What did that have to do with anything? "Yes, I sent you the email. I wanted to ask you about Marcus's alibi—"

"Are your parents there?" Mr. Miller interrupted.

"Um, no," I said. "They're at work." Grandma was in the living room watching a show.

"I see. Well, maybe you should have one of them call me back. I'm very busy."

"I'm trying to find Marcus's alibi witness," I said. "Marcus already told me her name is Susan Thomas, but I'm having trouble finding her. Did you look for her during his trial? I thought you could help me. Or if you can share anything with me about the case, that would be helpful. Marcus told me he's innocent, and I'm trying to—"

"Listen," Mr. Miller interrupted again. He sounded exasperated. "I really don't have time for this. The case is closed. You're, what, Marcus's relative or something?"

"I'm . . ." I swallowed. "I'm his daughter." I'd never actually said those words about Marcus before.

"Oh." Mr. Miller's voice softened a little. "Look, I'm sorry, that's gotta be really hard for you. I wish I had better news, but he already appealed his verdict and lost." I heard him shuffling paper through the phone. "He could still get out on parole, though."

My eyes filled with tears, but I tried not to sound like I was upset. "So that's it? You can't help me?"

"I'm sorry. I have another call right now so I'd better—"

I hung up the phone before he could finish.

I pressed my palms over my eyes as tears squeezed out of them. Mr. Miller probably still thought Marcus was guilty, so of course he wouldn't help me. Maybe this was all a lost cause.

But there was a tiny voice in the back of my brain. It told me to remember what I read in *The Wrongfully*

Convicted, and in my research about the Innocence Project. It told me that Susan Thomas was out there somewhere, and she still might've seen Marcus that day. It told me not to lose hope. Not yet.

Now that I'd gotten my cereal cupcake recipe right, it was time to experiment with the food coloring. On Saturday, I separated the batch into three different bowls and mixed a little gel food coloring into each one—red, blue, and green, to match the Froot Loops. The batter looked super vibrant. I scooped a little of each color batter into each cupcake pan before baking them.

The first batch came out pretty enough, but I realized I could've used a toothpick to swirl the colored batter a little so the finished cupcakes looked more tie-dyed.

I started working on another batch of cupcake batter so I could try that, when my phone chirped.

It had to be Susan Thomas! I wiped my hands on my apron and grabbed my phone.

It *was* a reply from Susan Thomas, and I skimmed through the email, looking for Marcus's name. But it wasn't good news. She said she only moved to Brookline eight years earlier, so she wasn't living there when Marcus would've gone to a tag sale. She wasn't the right person.

My shoulders slumped as I put my phone down. I was back at square one.

When I heard Trevor come home that night, I texted him to come over so I could show him the email.

"This is hopeless," I told him.

"Are you sure you don't know anything else about her? Can you ask Marcus again?"

"All Marcus said he remembered is her name, what she looked like, the fact that she lived in Brookline, and she mentioned students at one point. Oh, and she was married, with no kids."

"I have an idea." Trevor pulled my laptop toward him and opened a search browser. He typed in "Susan Thomas Brookline MA professor."

"Oh." My eyes lit up.

"There are so many colleges in Boston," Trevor said. "Maybe she teaches at one of them."

"That makes sense." I wished I'd thought of it.

Unlike the other times we searched for Susan Thomas, this time the results got smaller—the first page was all websites about the same person. The first link was to a Harvard University page for a Professor Susan Thomas who worked in the math department, and below that was a résumé website for the same person.

Trevor clicked on the first link.

"There's a picture." I stared at the small rectangular box that appeared next to the professor's biography. The picture was in black and white, but it was clear that she had dark hair and dark eyes. I squinted at it. "Does it look like she has freckles?"

Trevor leaned in to the picture himself. "I'm not sure. Let's read her bio."

The two of us stared at the computer screen as we read it. Right there in the first line, it said that she was a Massachusetts native.

"So she grew up here," Trevor said.

"But it doesn't say whether or not she lived in Brookline," I pointed out. "What about the other website that came up below this one? The résumé one—it might say where she's lived."

Trevor clicked back over to the website and we stared at her résumé. There, at the bottom, under education, it said Brookline High School.

"She lived in Brookline!" I said. "It has to be her!"

"It says she went to high school there," Trevor said. "She must've grown up there. But Marcus said she was in her thirties when he met her."

"Right, but maybe she lived there for a while after. Or moved back, or something."

"Yeah," Trevor said.

I switched back to the Harvard page. I scrolled down and found a list of classes that Professor Thomas would teach when the fall semester started in a few weeks.

"Do you see this?" I asked, still staring at the screen. "Classes start up at Harvard on August thirtieth. School doesn't start for us until September sixth. Maybe one of those days in between, we can go to Harvard and talk to her, figure out if she's the same person Marcus met. And if she is, I can see if she remembers him."

Trevor nodded. "But how will we get to Harvard without your parents finding out what we're going there for? Maybe you should try emailing her first."

"You're right."

I opened my email and wrote out a similar message to the one I'd sent the first Susan Thomas. "Let's hope she replies faster than the last one."

Chapter Twenty-Five

I needed a plan. It'd been a few days since I sent the email to Professor Thomas, and still no response.

"I'm tired of waiting for her email," I told Trevor. We were sitting at the bottom of our porch steps one afternoon, eating orange Popsicles after riding our bikes around the neighborhood. Well, Trevor was eating his Popsicle. A few seconds earlier, my phone chirped and I dropped my Popsicle while trying to get to my pocket as fast as possible. Butternut was on it in a second, happily licking it while I checked the email—which turned out to be spam. I wanted to throw my phone on the ground, too, but Trevor stopped me. I put it in my pocket instead and debated going inside to get another Popsicle.

"Can you call her office at Harvard?" Trevor asked, keeping his voice low so Grandma wouldn't hear us from inside.

"If I have to." I opened the Harvard website on my phone and searched for Professor Thomas's name. I found her phone number on her department's page.

I tapped my finger on the number so my phone would start calling and then quickly put it to my ear before I could change my mind. It started ringing, so I got up and walked a few steps away from the house so Grandma definitely couldn't hear.

Ring.

Ring.

Ring.

"Hello, you've reached the office of Professor Susan Thomas in the Harvard University math department. I'm away from my desk, so please leave a message, and I will get back to you as soon as I can. Thank you, and have a nice day."

There was a beep at the end, so I had to think fast. "Uh, hi, um, Professor Thomas. This is Zoe Washington. I sent you an email last week, asking if you knew a man named Marcus Johnson. He said he met you thirteen years ago at your tag sale? I put his picture in the email, so can you please let me know if you recognize him? It's really important." I gave her my email address and phone number before thanking her and ending the call.

I'd gotten a little sweaty from the bike ride, but now I was drenched in sweat from talking on the phone.

I'd earned a second Popsicle.

"Do you think she's ignoring me?" I asked Trevor a couple of days later. I stood on the edge of the driveway while he practiced shooting his basketball into the net above the garage.

He dribbled the ball for a few seconds and then took a shot. The basketball hit the rim of the net but then went in. "Maybe your email went into her junk folder," Trevor said.

"And my voice mail too?"

He bit his lip. "I don't know. Maybe she heard how young you were and didn't want to get involved."

"Well, that's rude."

"Yeah."

I kicked a pebble with my foot. "This is so annoying. If she's going to ignore my messages, then we have to go find her. She'll definitely be around when classes start again next week. This is our chance. She won't be able to ignore me if I'm right in front of her face."

Trevor took another shot before asking, "But how are we going to convince our parents to let us go there without telling them why?"

"We won't tell them. We'll go without them knowing."

But how?

"How about this," I told Trevor, standing closer to him and speaking even softer. "We'll tell our parents that we want to ride our bikes. Then we ride to Davis Square, take the T to Harvard Square, and then walk to Harvard's campus. If we time it right, we can get there before her class ends. Then I can show her Marcus's picture, see if she remembers him—which hopefully she will. And then I'll finally know."

"Do you think they'll really let us be gone for that long?" Trevor asked.

"How long do you think it would take all together, for us to get to Harvard and back?" I asked.

Trevor pulled out his phone and opened the map app, so we could calculate our route. We decided we needed three hours to do everything.

I smiled. "Three hours isn't bad! But that's too long for a bike ride. Let me think." I paced our driveway while Trevor shot the basketball into the hoop a few more times. He missed the first couple of shots, but made the last one.

I snatched the basketball from Trevor as an idea came to me.

"Hey!" he said.

"What if we ask our parents to go to the movie theater in Davis," I said. "We can tell them we also want to get ice cream at the J.P. Licks. If they drop us off, we won't even need our bikes, which will give us more time."

Trevor smiled. "Good idea. I bet they'd let us hang out in Davis for a few hours."

"Yeah." Mom let me hang out at the mall alone before, with Jasmine and Maya. Davis Square, with all its restaurants and college students walking around, seemed like a safe place for us to spend a few hours. Hopefully our parents agreed. "Okay. Ask your parents tonight if we can go next Thursday. Professor Thomas's class is from twelve to one thirty, so if we get to Davis at twelve thirty, that should be enough time to find her class before it ends."

"My mom works the night shift on Thursdays, so she can probably drive us. We have to make sure we get back to Davis when she comes to pick us up," Trevor said. "Or we're dead."

"We'll totally be back in time," I said with confidence.

"We know exactly what we're doing, and exactly where we need to go. This is going to work!"

The real worry that was lodged deep in my throat was that all this sneaking around wouldn't be worth it in the end. That we wouldn't find what we were looking for— the truth about Marcus's innocence. Then I wouldn't know if Marcus was lying to me.

But I had to stay optimistic.

I was still holding Trevor's basketball, so I dribbled it a couple of times. Then I took a shot. It went right into the basket.

"Nice," Trevor said. "Lucky shot."

I turned to him and grimaced. "What do you mean, lucky?"

"I don't know," Trevor said. "I thought . . . I mean, I didn't think you liked basketball. Or any sports. You always complain about gym class."

"That's because some people in gym class stink," I said. "I can't even trip *by accident* without *some people* making a big deal about it." I didn't bring up Lincoln tripping me on purpose again, but the way Trevor looked down at his feet made it clear that he knew what I was talking about. "I like sports better when I can play with my friends."

I picked up the basketball again and made another shot. It sailed right in. Nothin' but net.

"Whoa," Trevor said, his eyes wide.

"How's that for lucky?" I said, grinning. "You know, Marcus used to play basketball as a kid. He was really good, apparently."

"Really?" Trevor said. "That's cool."

"Anyway, I don't *not* like basketball," I said. "You never asked me to play with you. It seemed like you only wanted to play with your brother or other friends."

"Sorry. I didn't know." Trevor went over and picked up the ball, then tentatively asked, "Want to play some more right now?"

I smiled. "Sure."

We played a couple rounds of horse until our parents got home from work and we had to stop for dinner. We agreed to text each other after we asked our parents about going to Davis Square.

This plan could be a total failure, but at least I had Trevor back.

Chapter Twenty-Six

It was just Mom and me for dinner, since Dad had to work late. She'd brought home Thai food takeout, and we both had plates with pad thai and spring rolls in front of us. So far, it'd been the quietest dinner ever, which was fine by me. I didn't have anything to say to Mom. Well, except for one thing I still had to ask her.

I swirled more noodles around my fork and came out with it. "Can I go to Davis Square with Trevor on Thursday?" I asked. "We want to watch a movie."

"Oh." She sounded surprised. "I can take you over the weekend."

I shook my head. "It has to be Thursday."

Mom reached for the bottle of sriracha and squeezed some more on her pad thai. "Why?"

"There's a group going—other kids from school will be there. As, like, an end-of-summer thing." I paused, and then added, "I mean, twelve seems old enough to watch a movie with only my friends."

Mom narrowed her eyes. "Let me think about it."

"Please? Davis Square is crowded during the day. There will be lots of people around. The ice cream place is right across the street from the movie theater. We want to go there after the movie."

"Who else will be there?" Mom asked.

"Um." I thought fast. "It's a couple of Trevor's friends. From basketball. Now that Trevor and I are friends again, I'm going to try to get to know them." The lies rolled off my tongue so easily, which made the pit in my stomach grow.

"What about Maya? Is she back home yet?"

"She won't be home until the weekend after," I said.

Mom stared at me for what felt like an eternity, and then said, "You will only go inside the movie theater, and then right across the street to the ice cream shop. No walking around anywhere else."

"Yes!" I tried not to show how excited I was. "Trevor said his mom could drive us." I wasn't sure if he'd gotten permission yet, but I hoped he had.

"All right," Mom finally said. "You must have your phone on the entire time, on vibrate when the movie is playing, so if there's an emergency, we can reach each other."

"Okay."

Normally this was the part when I'd give her a hug, but for some reason, it felt weird. Awkward. The Marcus stuff was taking up space between us. So I just said "Thank you" and finished eating my pad thai.

When I got back to my room after dinner, I texted Trevor.

Me: Mom said I can go to Davis for a few hours without a chaperone!

Trevor: Mine too! She can drive us.

Our plan was a go.

The day before our Great Harvard Adventure—GHA for short, as I liked to call it—another letter from Marcus arrived.

To my Little Tomato,
I'm so glad we got a chance to talk on the phone—not once, but twice. It was so great to

hear your voice out loud. I think this good mood will last me awhile!

I don't know what you're planning, now that you have my alibi witness's name, but I hope you don't get yourself into any trouble. What I want most is for you to live a happy life, and not have to worry about me being in prison. Just enjoy being a kid, okay?

Summer is almost over. You're going into the seventh grade, right? How do you feel about that? When I was in middle school, I always liked math class, strange as that sounds. I found it satisfying to solve all of those equations, like they were puzzles.

Before I go, here's another song for your playlist: "To Zion," by Lauryn Hill.

Love,

Marcus

I listened to the song after reading the letter, but decided not to write back right away. I wanted to wait to see what happened the next day. If everything worked out, I'd have some good news to share.

The next morning, I woke up early and packed my backpack, making sure I had everything Trevor and

I needed. There was my journal, with all the notes I'd taken about Marcus's case and Professor Thomas. I'd written down details about her class, like what time it ended and what building it was held in. I'd also printed a map of the campus and circled where we'd enter it and where her building was.

I was also bringing my picture of Marcus, and at the last second, I stuffed his letters in between pages of my journal too. I wasn't sure I needed to take them with me. It's not like Professor Thomas would need to see them or anything, but I felt better having them. They were a reminder of why I was doing this in the first place.

The night before, while my parents were watching TV, I snuck into the kitchen to make snacks. I made two peanut butter and jelly sandwiches—one for me, and one for Trevor. I also grabbed a couple of apples from the counter and two bottles of water. I didn't want Mom to see the food, since I was only supposed to be seeing a movie and getting ice cream while I was gone. So I stuffed everything into my backpack underneath a sweatshirt. I normally brought one to movie theaters in case I got cold, so Mom wouldn't find that weird.

When my parents left for work, instead of Grandma coming over, I went to Trevor's house to hang out until it was time for us to head to Davis Square for our "movie."

Trevor's mom's shift didn't start until that night, so she was going to drop us off and pick us up.

In his bedroom, I showed Trevor everything I'd packed in my backpack for our adventure, and we went over our plan—quietly, so his mom wouldn't hear us.

At noon, Patricia poked her head into his room. "Ready to go?"

We went outside and got into her car. Trevor sat in the front passenger seat next to his mom and I sat behind the driver's seat.

"Excited for the movie?" Patricia asked once she pulled out of the driveway.

"Yup!" I said. Trevor glanced back at me and I smiled at him.

"I can't believe how fast you're growing up. I remember when you two would watch a movie together curled up on blankets in our living room. Now you're going off on your own, meeting friends." Her voice got all nostalgic. "I know middle school can be tough, but this is the beginning of such a fun time for you two. Your first taste of independence."

"You're not gonna cry, are you?" Trevor asked his mother, sounding annoyed.

"Of course not," Patricia said, though her voice did

sound a little like she was holding back tears. "Anyway, the movie starts at one, right?"

"Yup," Trevor said right away. "We're meeting our other friends inside the theater. Whoever gets there first is supposed to save seats for the rest of us."

"Right," I said, impressed at how easily Trevor lied to his mom. Maybe I was rubbing off on him. I was glad I'd decided to give him another chance, and that he was coming with me today. There was no way I could do this alone.

The drive to Davis Square took only five minutes. Trevor's mom pulled in front of the Somerville Theatre, which was an old-timey theater that still had some of its original features. The words "Somerville Theatre" were engraved in stone on the front of the building. The marquee didn't have screens with electronic letters—instead, it had black letters that had to be stuck to the sign. Every time a movie changed, someone had to stand up on a ladder and switch them by hand.

"All right, kids. This is your stop." Patricia looked at me in the rearview mirror. "You have your ticket money, Zoe?"

"Yup." Mom had given me thirty dollars that morning, to pay for my ticket, some popcorn if I wanted it, and ice cream, with a little extra in case of an emergency. I planned to use some of it to pay for my CharlieTicket to ride the T. I also had some of my leftover birthday money, in case we needed it. If things in Harvard Square took too long, we could take a cab back to Davis Square. Or, if we got everything done fast, we could get back to Davis early and actually get some ice cream at J.P. Licks before Trevor's mom came to pick us up.

"Bye, Mom," Trevor said, and we both got out of the car.

"Text me when the movie's over, so I know you're heading to the ice cream shop, okay?" Patricia said.

I could see from the expression on Trevor's face that he was trying to figure out exactly what time to text his mom so she would think he'd gotten out of the movie.

"Will do," Trevor told her.

Patricia kept her car parked at the curb and watched us to make sure we got inside the movie theater okay. Even though we didn't have any time to waste, we went into the theater and pretended to get in line for tickets. I hoped we didn't have to stand there for too long and actually buy tickets. What if Patricia waited until our nonexistent group of friends arrived?

"Is she still watching us?" I asked, keeping my eyes on the front of the line so we didn't look suspicious.

Next to me, Trevor peeked over his shoulder. "Nah, she's gone."

I smiled. I couldn't believe it worked, and we were actually alone in Davis Square. Hopefully the rest of our plan would go as smoothly. "Let's go," I said. "The sooner we can get to Harvard Square, the better."

Chapter Twenty-Seven

Trevor and I left the theater and walked half a block to the T station. Since it was early afternoon on a weekday, when everyone was at work, it wasn't crowded. Thank goodness, because it was already overwhelming to be doing this by ourselves. We took the escalator down into the station and walked to the ticket machine.

"Have you done this before?" I asked Trevor. I should've paid more attention when my parents bought CharlieTickets.

"No, but it looks pretty easy." He reached into his cargo shorts pocket and took out some cash.

While he pressed a few buttons on the screen, I peered

around the station. There were painted tiles on the wall with what looked like kid drawings of faces, boats, and animals.

I was admiring them when I heard Trevor say, "Uhh . . ."

"What?" I glanced back at him and he was trying to put bills into the machine, but it wouldn't accept them.

He tried again. "It's not taking my money. I don't get it."

"Maybe because it's so wrinkled." It was like he'd crumpled the bills up into a ball before stuffing them into his pocket. "Let me try." I grabbed the money from him and quickly smoothed out the dollar bills. I held my breath as I tried inserting them again, but the machine spit them right out.

I groaned. "Let me use my cash." But by the time I reached into my backpack for it, the ticket screen had reset itself and we had to start all over.

"Ugh," I said. "This is so frustrating. We're wasting time."

"Maybe we should go to the ticket guy over there instead," Trevor said. "It might be faster."

"Okay."

We went to the ticket booth, where a man in a Red Sox hat was talking to the ticket guy. They seemed around the same age—older than my parents—and I wondered if they knew each other, because they were laughing about something. I couldn't think of anything funny about buying a train ticket.

Trevor and I stood behind them, waiting for them to be done. But whatever they were talking about must've been super interesting, because they kept on talking.

"This is taking forever," I mumbled under my breath as I bounced on my heels.

Then I heard a train rumble into the station one level below us.

"Great, we're missing a train," I said, glancing at my watch. We'd been in the station almost ten minutes already.

"There'll be another one," Trevor said.

I couldn't take it anymore. I cleared my throat really loudly—so loud, the sound echoed in the station.

The two men peered back at us.

"Whoops, sorry," the man talking to the ticket guy said. "Hey, man, it was nice seeing you," he said to the ticket guy. Then with a quick wave, he left.

Trevor and I hurried up to the counter and asked for four rides—two to get us to Harvard Square and two to get us back. The ticket guy didn't blink an eye at Trevor's crumpled bills.

After he handed us our passes, we hurried over to the ticket gate. Right then, I heard another train come into the station.

"Hurry!" I said to Trevor. He inserted the ticket and went through the gate. Then he handed it to me and I did the same.

We rushed to the escalator that led down to the track, and ran down it right as the train doors opened. We stepped onto the train right in time, and collapsed into two empty seats.

The doors closed and the train got moving. We were finally on our way, and I began to relax. I took my backpack off and put it near my feet. Trevor leaned over to retie one of his shoelaces.

Then there was a ding, and an automated voice said, "The next stop is Alewife."

"Alewife?" I repeated. "Oh no!"

"What?" Trevor asked, looking up from his sneaker.

"This train is going the wrong way. We need to go the other direction!" We'd wanted the inbound train, going toward Harvard Square and Boston, but had gotten on an outbound train instead.

"We'll turn around at the next stop," Trevor said.

"Yeah, and waste even more time." I leaned over and buried my face in my hands.

"Don't worry," Trevor said, elbowing me. "We still have plenty of time."

When we got to the Alewife station, we hurried onto the platform and went to the other side, where the train we needed would pull in. It smelled gross down there, like pee or something. Thankfully, it didn't take long for our train to arrive. When it pulled in, we hopped on and I took a seat right by the door. Trevor sat next to me.

We were quiet as the train started moving.

"The next stop is Davis Square," the automated voice said. Right where we started. I groaned.

I could barely sit still. I was on the edge of my seat, my legs ready to jump up and carry me off the train as soon as we arrived at Harvard Square. I checked the time on my phone. It'd been almost a half hour since we were dropped off in Davis. We only had two and a half hours before Patricia would expect us back at J.P. Licks.

"What if we can't find Professor Thomas in time?" I asked Trevor, wringing my hands together.

"We'll find her," he said. "She'll be teaching her class."

"Yeah." I forced my muscles to relax into the train seat. Lying to my parents about sending letters was one thing, but what we were doing now was way too stressful. I couldn't imagine how angry they'd be if they found out Trevor and I were on the T going to Harvard Square by ourselves. But if the rest of our plan went okay, it would be worth it.

Trevor took his phone out and started playing his Mario game as the train stopped back at Davis Square, then at Porter Station, where some people got off and on. Then the doors closed again. "The next stop is Harvard Square," said the train voice.

I grabbed Trevor's knee again and gripped it hard.

"Ow!" he said.

"Sorry." I sat on my hand instead.

The ride from Porter to Harvard Square felt way too long. When I could finally see the station outside the train windows, I got up and stood right in front of the door. Trevor stood behind me. The train seemed to inch its way into the station, and I wanted to scream at the conductor to hurry up already. Finally, the train stopped, and as soon as the doors opened, I sprinted off.

I wasn't exactly sure which way to go, so my eyes darted to the various signs on the walls. The people who got off the train with us all started walking in the same direction, so we followed them. We ended up in the main part of the station, which had a coffee place, newsstand, and several ticket machines.

The Harvard Square station was much busier than the other stations we'd been in. We had to weave our way around people to get to the escalator that led up to the street level.

Stepping outside felt like walking into a hot oven. Sun glared in my eyes, making me wish I'd remembered to bring my sunglasses. There were tons of people hanging around Harvard Square, especially right around where we walked outside. It was noisy—cars honking, people shouting, music blaring from somewhere down the street. There was a sunken sidewalk area near the train entrance, next to the Cambridge Information Center and another newsstand. A bunch of people sat on the benches and brick steps. One girl played a guitar and sang as people dropped dollars into the box at her feet. A skateboarder did a kick flip and almost rolled into me. I noticed lots of different-colored hair—blue, purple, fire orange, and one girl with thick, beautiful braids. It was a lot to take in, but we had no time.

"Which way do we go?" Trevor asked.

I'd been to Harvard Square enough times with my parents. Harvard's campus was right in the center. Getting inside was the easy part. But we had to find the right building. I pulled out the campus map I'd printed. "This way."

Trevor followed me across a street and down the block that ran alongside campus. We quickly found a gate, walked under its tall brick archway, and ended up on a small quad. It was calmer and quieter there. "I think these are all dorms," I said, glancing down at my map. "We need to go farther into campus to find the building we want—Sever Hall."

I hurried down a path that led past the dorms and into the next quad. This one was larger—on the map, it was called Old Yard. It was so pretty. The grass was super green, and the brick buildings looked majestic in the sunshine. It was exactly what you'd think of when you imagined a college campus. Some students were walking around and others sat at small tables on the grass. A large tour group was a few steps ahead of us. A bunch of trees blocked some of the sun, so it was cooler there. I wished I could walk around and take my time looking at everything, even piggyback on the tour, but there was no time.

We had a professor to find—and quick.

Chapter Twenty-Eight

I looked down at my map again. "Sever Hall is in the next quad over—Harvard Yard. This way." I pulled Trevor's arm and we hurried across this quad, between another couple of buildings, and into Harvard Yard. It looked similar to the other quad, with lots of trees and people hanging around.

Sever Hall was on the other end. I recognized the huge redbrick building from photos online. It looked sort of like an old castle, with dozens of windows and an archway entrance. "That's it," I told Trevor, and we hurried over to it. I felt lighter all of a sudden. We made it! I couldn't believe we were there.

Trevor was checking his watch when I glanced over at him. "It's only one ten," he said. "We found the building faster than we thought. There's still twenty minutes before her class ends."

My stomach grumbled, and I thought of the sandwiches and apples in my backpack.

"Want to sit here and eat lunch?" I asked.

"Okay," Trevor said.

We walked over to two bright-yellow metal chairs in the middle of the quad. I took out the food and handed one of everything to Trevor.

"Thanks." He started eating. "Did you pack any of your cereal cupcakes?"

I shook my head.

"I want to try them sometime."

"Okay," I said. "But I'm warning you, there's no chocolate in them."

"That's okay," he said. "I'm sure they're still good. Everything you bake is good. You're going to win *Kids Bake Challenge!*"

I laughed. "I haven't even auditioned yet."

"I know." He smiled.

I opened my bottle of water and took a big swig. I unwrapped the sandwich, but now my stomach was churning and I wasn't sure I could eat.

Trevor finished the first half of his sandwich and looked over at me. "Why aren't you eating?"

I shrugged. "I can't eat. I'm really scared all of a sudden."

"Scared of what?"

"I don't know. If this professor is the correct Susan Thomas, then she's right in that building, and in a few minutes, I'm going to know whether or not Marcus was telling me the truth. Whether he's really innocent of murder."

"Isn't that what you want?" Trevor asked while chewing.

"Yeah, but what if I show her the picture and she says she's never seen him before?" The idea alone made my eyes water with tears. I blinked to make them go away.

Trevor looked like he wasn't sure what to say. "It'll be okay."

"I don't want Marcus to be guilty. I don't want him to be a murderer. He doesn't have to be my dad—Paul's my dad—but I still want him to be my friend. But not if he's really a lying monster."

Trevor nodded. "You don't know anything yet. Professor Thomas might remember him."

"I hope so." I smiled and wiped my eyes. "How much more time do we have before her class gets out?"

Trevor peered at his watch and then jumped to his

feet. "Only five more minutes."

"Oh." I stood up, still holding my uneaten sandwich. I took a couple of quick bites to quiet my still-grumbling stomach and chased them down with another swig of water. I put the rest of our food back inside my backpack. "Let's go inside and find her classroom. It's room 215."

We walked inside the building and were blasted with cold air-conditioning. "This way," I said once I spotted the staircase.

We walked up to the second floor and found our way to room 215. The door was closed, but there was a small window on it. I took a deep breath. This was it.

My whole body shook as I walked up to the window and peeked inside. There was a woman at the front of the room, standing in front of a chalkboard that had a bunch of math equations on it. It may as well have been in another language. I counted the students and reached the number ten. They sat at desks, taking notes as the teacher spoke.

As I stared at the woman, something in my brain told me that she seemed younger than the picture we'd seen online. And her hair was shorter.

Trevor came up behind me and peered into the window himself. "Is that her?" he asked. "She looks different."

I started to panic. "Are we sure this is the right room?" I moved away from the door and put my backpack on the hallway floor. I took out my journal and flipped open to the page where I'd written down the details of Professor Thomas's class. It said it right there—Sever Hall, room 215, from 12:00 to 1:30 on Thursdays, starting that same day. We were definitely in the right place.

"Class is ending," Trevor said. "They're putting their notebooks away and stuff."

My heart sped up. "What do we do?"

Before Trevor had the chance to answer, the door swung open and a few students filed out. And the next thing I knew, Trevor was walking inside the classroom.

Chapter Twenty-Nine

"What are you doing?" I hissed at Trevor, but he was already gone. I threw my journal back into my backpack and followed him into the classroom. Trevor was walking up to the teacher—who, now that I was closer, I realized couldn't possibly be Professor Thomas. This person looked only a few years older than the students who'd just walked out of the room. There's no way she was in her thirties when she had a tag sale twelve years earlier.

I wanted to throw up. We'd made it all the way out to Harvard Square without our parents, and we still may not have found the person we were looking for.

"Hi," Trevor said to the teacher. "Is this Professor Thomas's class?"

The teacher, who was busy putting her laptop and folders into her messenger bag, looked up, surprised to see a twelve-year-old boy standing in front of her, and me a few feet behind watching the two of them.

"Uh, yes," she said.

"Are you Professor Thomas?" Trevor asked.

She laughed, as if Trevor had asked the funniest question ever. "No. I'm her TA."

"TA?" Trevor asked.

"Teaching assistant. Professor Thomas had to leave a little early today, so I taught the rest of class."

My chest filled with a huge bubble of disappointment. We'd failed. My one shot to find her, and she wasn't there.

"Are you looking for her for some reason?" the TA asked, wrinkling her eyebrows at Trevor.

"Yes," Trevor said. "Do you know where she is?"

"She had an important phone call. I think she went back to her office for it."

"Where's that?" Trevor asked.

"The math department is in the science building," the TA said. "Her office is on the third floor, to the right of the stairs. Her name's on the door."

I glanced up at the clock in the classroom. We only had twenty minutes before we had to head home, and now we had to go to a whole other building to talk to Professor Thomas—if she was even there at all.

"Thanks!" Trevor told the TA, and then he turned to me.

"There isn't enough time," I said, about to start crying again. Harvard's campus was big, and I had no idea where the science building was, or how long it'd take to walk there.

"If we run, there is." He grabbed my arm and pulled me out of the classroom. "Let's go!"

He was right. There was still a chance—we could still find Professor Thomas. Adrenaline burst through me as we raced back down the stairs of Sever Hall and back outside. Once we were on the quad again, Trevor asked for my campus map, which I'd forgotten all about. I pulled it out of my backpack and he scanned it for a second.

"I found it," he said, pointing to a building on the map. It wasn't one of the buildings in the quad we were on, but it didn't look that far. We had to go back to the Old Yard and across an area called the Plaza.

We took off running again, past students reading on the quad, weaving around a tour group and in between buildings, until we got to the Plaza. By then, I was sweating and panting. My phone said we still had fifteen minutes to talk to her. That had to be enough time.

The science building wasn't as majestic as the ones in the quads. It was a regular stone building with a bunch of windows. Above the entrance in big letters were the words "Science Center." We ran up to the doors and went inside.

We found the stairs and ran up to the third floor, bumping into students and professors who gave us strange looks as we passed. We stopped short at the door to the right of the stairway. There on a sign on the door were the words "Professor Susan Thomas, Mathematics."

"We made it," I said between breaths. "Hopefully she's in there. Here goes . . ." I took a deep breath and knocked on the door. Then I stopped breathing as I waited to hear a sound from inside.

Seconds passed, which felt like years. Finally, a voice called from the other side of the door.

"Come in," it said. A woman's voice.

I beamed at Trevor and he beamed back. *We did it*, I thought. *We found her.*

I opened the door carefully, like if I did it too fast, the person on the other side would disappear.

A woman sat behind a desk, which had a computer

and several piles of paper. I studied her face, and it was her. She looked just like her picture. My throat went dry.

She gave us a smile that looked nice but confused at the same time. I was getting used to people looking at Trevor and me, wondering what we were doing in places where kids usually didn't go.

"Can I help you?" she asked.

I didn't say anything. My mind went completely blank. Then Trevor nudged me, which jolted me back into action. I slipped my backpack off my back and it made a thud when it hit the floor.

"Yes. You're Professor Thomas, right?" I unzipped the main pocket of my backpack, not wasting any time.

She nodded and smiled again. "Yes, that's me. Can I help you with something?"

I almost burst into tears when she said she was the person we were looking for. But I stopped myself and focused on what I was there to do.

"I'm Zoe Washington," I said as I fumbled through my backpack and yanked my journal out of it. I quickly flipped through the pages and pulled out the picture of Marcus. "I emailed you about this but I don't know if you got it. I also left a voice mail." I walked to Professor Thomas's desk with the picture held out in front of me. "Do you recognize this person?" I put the picture down right in front of her, on top of some papers with numbers and equations on it.

Recognition flashed in Professor Thomas's eyes. "I'm behind on emails, but yes—I did get your voice mail. I'm sorry I didn't reply right away. It's been a hectic start of the school year." She then peered down at the photo and frowned at it. "Remind me how I should know this man?" She looked up at me.

"His name is Marcus Johnson," I said. "You met him over twelve years ago when he came to your house to buy a futon. You were moving out of your house and you talked on the phone the day before. Do you remember him?"

Professor Thomas looked at me with a confused expression, but then she glanced at the picture on her desk and picked it up to get a closer look. Her mouth pinched as she stared at it.

C'mon. You have to recognize him. There was a clock on the wall above the window behind her. We had to be back in Davis Square in forty minutes. My mind raced. *C'mon, c'mon, remember.*

Finally, Professor Thomas sighed and put the picture down. "I'm sorry. Maybe he looks a little familiar, but I'm really not sure. You say I met him at my house? What's his name again?"

"Marcus Johnson. He's my dad. My . . . biological dad. And he's . . ." I swallowed hard. "He's in prison right now. For something he didn't do. At least, he says he didn't do it. I don't know if he's telling the truth." Now I was crying a little. I couldn't help it. It seemed so hopeless, the idea that he could be innocent. I was probably naive to think he didn't deserve to be in prison. "He says he was at your house looking at the futon you were selling when the crime happened. I'm here to find out if he's telling the truth. If he really is innocent."

Professor Thomas's eyes widened and she pushed a box of tissues from the corner of her desk closer to me. I took one and blew my nose with it.

"I've had a few tag sales over the years," Professor Thomas said. "But I don't specifically remember meeting your father. His name doesn't ring any bells. I'm really sorry."

"Maybe you talked about music? He likes Stevie Wonder and Boyz II Men and Jill Scott. Also, he was going to college at the time—UMass Boston. He played basketball, too, and liked to cook." I tried to remember what else I knew about Marcus, so I could describe him to Professor Thomas better. But I hadn't even met him in person. I still knew so little about him.

Professor Thomas frowned. "I don't know . . ."

It was a lost cause. "Okay," I said, wiping more tears from my face. "Sorry for bothering you."

The way Professor Thomas looked at me, I could tell she felt sorry for me. "That's all right. I'm sorry I can't help you."

I turned toward the door and took a couple of steps toward it.

But Trevor didn't follow behind me. "Excuse me," he said to Professor Thomas. "I'm Trevor, Zoe's friend. Can we give you Zoe's email address again? In case you remember Marcus?"

I turned to see Professor Thomas's reaction. She appeared surprised by Trevor's question, but then she reached for a notepad and pen on her desk and handed it to Trevor. "Sure, write down your email address or phone number and I'll let you know if I remember anything. Can I see the picture again, before you go?"

I walked to the desk and showed the picture to her again. While she stared at it, I wrote down my email address and cell number on the notepad, which Trevor handed to me. When I looked up at Professor Thomas again, she was shaking her head. "Gosh, I really wish I could help you more." She handed the photo back, and I gave her the notepad. She glanced down at my contact information. "I'll be in touch if I happen to remember something."

I nodded and said thank you.

"Good luck," she said as Trevor and I left her office.

We walked down the stairs and out of the building, both of us at a loss for words.

Chapter Thirty

My shoulders slumped as I stood outside the science building and stared at the students walking around, going to and from class. While they went about their day like everything was normal, all I wanted to do was cry and scream and throw something.

Marcus had told me not to look for Professor Thomas because he didn't want me to get my hopes up. Probably because he knew I wouldn't find anything, because his alibi was all a lie. Grandma had warned me about the same thing, because maybe deep down, she knew the truth, too. Why didn't I listen to them?

"I'm so stupid," I mumbled.

"You're not stupid," Trevor said. "You're one of the smartest people I know."

"I never should've trusted Marcus. He's guilty, that's the end of it. He's a big fat liar, and I never should've wasted my time. I'm done with him and his letters." Tears stung behind my eyelids, but I blinked them away.

"Um," Trevor said, his voice tentative. "I know you're sad and angry, and I get it, but we should probably run for the T. My mom is going to pick us up from Davis in fifteen minutes."

"Okay," I said, even though the last thing I wanted to do was run anywhere. But I knew that day would get a million times worse if we didn't get back to Davis Square in time, and our parents figured out that we weren't where we said we'd be.

I followed Trevor as he jogged out of Harvard's campus and back down the street toward the T station. Harvard Square was still crowded, even though it was after the lunch rush. By the time we got to the street, we couldn't jog anymore without going into the road, so we did our best to quickly dodge around people left and right.

Half a block from the station, a cab pulled over on our side of the street and let out a passenger—a woman wearing a patterned sundress. I gripped Trevor's arm and pointed to it.

"Do you think a cab would be faster than waiting for the next train?" I asked.

"Maybe. We have to decide right now, because it's about to leave."

Without a word, I ran to the cab and knocked on the window before the driver could pull off. Trevor was right behind me. The cab driver rolled down the window.

"Can you take us to Davis Square? I have cash," I said, hoping he wouldn't ignore me because I was a kid.

"Hop in," he said, and Trevor and I got into the back of the cab.

I buckled my seat belt and relaxed into the seat, happy we'd at least get back to Davis in time.

But a couple of minutes into the drive, I realized we might've made a big mistake.

"Should it be taking us this long just to get out of Harvard Square?" I asked Trevor as the cab crawled through traffic.

"I don't know," Trevor said. "Maybe the train would've been better after all."

"We're going to be late," I said. "And then our parents will find out we weren't at the movies, and I'll be grounded for life." Now, more than anything, I wanted to be home. I wanted this day to be over.

"We might still make it," Trevor said. "Maybe my

mom will be running late. She runs late sometimes."

When Trevor mentioned his mother, I remembered something. I sat up straight and looked at him with wide eyes. "Weren't you supposed to text her when we got out of the movie?" I made air quotes when I said the word "movie."

Trevor's mouth formed an O. "I totally forgot."

"We're so dead." I buried my face in my hands.

Trevor took out his phone. "I don't see any texts from her. She would've texted me if she was really mad," Trevor said. "Maybe she forgot about it."

"I hope so." I stared out the window.

It took another fifteen minutes for the cab to get us to Davis Square, which meant we were ten minutes late to meet Trevor's mom. We had the cab driver drop us off down the street from J.P. Licks. We paid him as fast as we could, jumped out of the cab, and started walking toward the ice cream shop.

"Do you see her?" I asked Trevor.

He searched up and down the street for his mom's blue car. The street was full of cars, which all blurred together. "I don't see her. I told you she's late sometimes."

I exhaled in relief. I couldn't believe we were getting away with this. It was the one consolation for what had turned out to be a pretty disappointing day.

"Let's go stand in front of J.P. Licks," Trevor said.

I nodded in agreement, and we started walking toward the corner so we could cross over to it.

But before we could do that, a car pulled into the parking spot beside us. The same blue car that we'd just looked for—Patricia's car. The passenger side window was rolled down and Patricia glared at us from the driver's seat. From the angry expression on her face, I knew what she was about to say wasn't good.

"Get in the car." She didn't yell it, but her tone told us we'd better listen to her. My heart started beating fast.

Without a word, Trevor and I jumped into the car.

I expected Trevor's mom to start driving us home right away, but she didn't. Instead, she twisted in her seat so that she faced both of us, giving each of us a hard look. "We're going to go home," she said calmly, "and then you are going to tell me *exactly* what you were up to this afternoon, when you were *not* watching a movie or getting ice cream. Don't even try to lie to me, because I just saw you get out of a taxi. Also, I know you weren't out with Lincoln and Sean like you told me, Trevor, because as I was leaving to come pick you up, they came by the house looking for you. I thought maybe I'd misremembered who you were going to the movie with, but now I know it was all a lie."

I was going to throw up. We were so busted. I tried to

think of a way to explain what we were doing in a cab, but I couldn't think of a single good lie. Trevor didn't have one either, or else he knew not to argue with his mother, because he didn't say anything.

I could see my mom's face already. She was going to be so angry. And disappointed in me, which would feel even worse. I had no idea what my punishment would be, but it would be bad.

I totally deserved it, too. Today was a fail. It turned out there was no good reason for me to lie to my family.

Trevor's mom started driving toward home, and then I heard a familiar chirping sound—my email alert. I took my cell phone out of my backpack pocket and opened my inbox.

I gasped. There was a new email from Professor Thomas. I couldn't get it open fast enough.

Date: September 1
From: Susan Thomas
To: Zoe Washington
Subject: I have your letter

Dear Zoe,
I found your letter on the floor of my office sometime after you left. I didn't notice it right away, but once I

did, I tried looking for you, but you were already gone. The letter must have fallen out of your bag. I apologize for reading the first few lines. I didn't know what it was at first. As soon as I realized it was yours, I stopped reading and emailed you. I would like to return it to you.

Also, I want to let you know that after seeing "Little Tomato" written on the top of the letter, I remembered something. I think I remember Marcus now. Please email me, or if you'd like, you can call my office line. The number is below, and I'll be here for the rest of the afternoon.

Sincerely,
Susan

Susan Thomas
Professor of Mathematics
Harvard University
617-555-1485

Chapter Thirty-One

I had to call Professor Thomas back. Fast.

The last time I got in trouble—for lying about what grade I got on a test—my parents took my phone away for a week. I was in way bigger trouble now, so I might never get my phone back.

But right as I tried to sneak the phone call from the back seat, Patricia pulled into our shared driveway. I looked up at the porch, and Grandma was standing there smiling at us, with Butternut happily wagging his tail at her feet. She couldn't know that Trevor and I had done something wrong. If she did, she wouldn't be smiling.

"Stay here. I'm going to talk to Zoe's grandmother," Patricia said before jumping out of the car.

"We're dead. Done. Burnt toast," Trevor said after his mom shut the car door behind her. His voice was full of dread, which made me feel terrible. It was my fault we were in this mess. Trevor sat very still in his seat and kept his eyes on his mother as she walked up the porch steps and began telling Grandma that she caught us getting out of a cab.

"Trevor, look at this." I shoved my phone toward him so he could see the email from Professor Thomas. But he wouldn't take the phone, or even turn around in his seat to face me.

"No. I don't want to get in more trouble." His voice was filled with worry.

"I'm really sorry we got caught. But look, Professor Thomas—"

I didn't get to finish my sentence because Patricia and Grandma were suddenly at the car. Patricia opened Trevor's door. "Let's go," she told him.

I glanced at Grandma, who stood by the passenger door with disbelief all over her face. She motioned for me to come with her, so I gripped my cell phone in one hand and got out of the car. Butternut jumped up my leg, so I reached down to pat his head. He licked my hand.

Then I looked over at Trevor, who followed Patricia up the porch steps with his head down.

"I called your mom," Grandma said. "She's coming home early to talk to you. I thought she should be the one to decide what happens next."

My body stiffened. This wasn't good. Mom never left work early unless I was sick and needed to be picked up from school, and even that didn't happen very much.

I followed Grandma into our house, and she motioned for me to take a seat on the living room couch. As I sat, I wedged my cell phone in the cushion behind me. If they couldn't find my phone, they couldn't take it away. Maybe I could tell them I lost it on the T . . . But, no. That was a lie, and honestly, I was tired of all the lying.

Butternut ran to the kitchen, probably for some water, and Grandma sat on the armchair across from me. "All right, Zoe, talk to me. Why did you lie about going to the movies? Where were you going in a cab?"

Before I could answer, though, Grandma kept talking. "What were you thinking? If you wanted to go somewhere, you could've asked me to take you. Instead you lied and got into a cab by yourself. You're smarter than that. You know how dangerous that was, getting into a car with a stranger. What if something had happened?"

I thought of the email from Professor Thomas, and how Grandma also thought Marcus was innocent. If I told her about it, she'd have to understand, and then she could help me explain it to my parents.

"I went to go see Susan Thomas," I said, but hearing the name only made Grandma wrinkle her eyebrows in confusion. "Marcus's alibi witness. She's a professor at Harvard."

Grandma's eyes widened. "Marcus's . . . We talked about this. You said you wouldn't go looking for this person. You went all the way to Harvard?"

"I know I said I wouldn't, but—"

"No, Zoe," Grandma said sternly. "I can't believe you lied to me. I'm very disappointed."

I frowned. "But I had to go . . ."

"You know what, save it for your mother. She'll be here in a few minutes." Grandma looked exhausted as she stared out of the front window. "I have to tell her about helping you write to Marcus." She shook her head. "I shouldn't even be surprised about your lying when I've been doing the same thing and setting a poor example. I never should've gone behind your parents' backs. This is my fault, too."

Guilt weighed down on me. It wasn't Grandma's fault that I went behind her back to find Professor Thomas.

And I was glad she let me keep writing to Marcus, since my life was better with him in it. But now Grandma felt bad. A huge lump formed in the back of my throat.

"I'm sorry that I lied to you, but I had no choice. I had to go see Professor Thomas, and I'm glad I did, because she remembers him. She remembers meeting Marcus!"

"She does?" Grandma asked, and I could see on her face that I'd caught her attention. "On the day Lucy was killed?"

"I think so. She didn't remember him at first, but she emailed me after I left her office. I need to call her back right now." I reached behind me and removed my phone from between the couch cushions.

Grandma sighed. "I can't let you do that. You can ask your mom when she gets here." She put her hand out. "Give me your phone."

I gripped it harder. "But she won't let me, I know it. Please, you have to help me."

"I've helped you enough." Grandma got up and stood in front of me. "The phone, Zoe."

"This is so unfair!" I yelled. I could feel my voice breaking. "If you really cared about me, you'd help me!"

Grandma pursed her lips and shook her head slightly.

"Ugh! I hate you!" I shouted. Right away, I wished I hadn't said it, but I was too angry to take it back.

She looked at me in disbelief, and then said, her voice quieter, "The phone."

I handed it to her and crossed my arms.

Grandma sat back down and I fumed silently. Then I heard Mom's car pull into our driveway. My stomach dropped.

Mom's heels clip-clopped against the porch steps and she opened the front door. Her mouth was set in a straight line as she focused her glare at me. I held my breath. I'd never seen her so angry.

I wiped my eyes and braced myself for her to start yelling at me, but before she could get a word out, Grandma started talking.

"Natalie, before you talk to Zoe, I have to confess something," she told Mom as she stood up from her seat, dropping my phone on the chair. I thought about jumping up to grab it but stopped myself, knowing it would only make things worse.

Mom glanced at her, shaking her head in confusion. "Can't it wait?"

"It has to do with why Zoe got in a cab this afternoon, so I think you should know." Grandma still didn't know about the T ride we'd taken, but I wasn't about to mention it.

Mom huffed in frustration. "Okay, what is it?"

Grandma took a deep breath. "For the past couple of months, I've helped Zoe send letters to Marcus. Now, before you—"

"You *what?*" Mom yelled, looking back and forth between Grandma and me. I kept my mouth shut.

"You had *no* right!" Mom said to Grandma.

Grandma crossed her arms. "A daughter should be able to know her father, even if he is in prison."

"*Father.*" Mom laughed. "You're kidding, right?"

"Now, listen. You never gave him a chance to be a dad to Zoe."

"As if you don't know why!" Mom said, lifting her hands in the air. "I mean, seriously, Mom."

I sat there watching them argue, not sure what else to do. At least Grandma hadn't mentioned that I actually spoke on the phone with Marcus. Twice.

"I know what Marcus is in prison for," Grandma said. "I never would've let him do anything to hurt Zoe. I read the letters he sent, and they were harmless."

Mom took a deep breath. "Let me get this straight. You went behind my back and gave Marcus's address in prison to Zoe?" she asked Grandma.

"He wrote to me first," I jumped in, my voice small. "He sent me a letter on my birthday, and I wrote him back. Grandma didn't find out until after I got his second letter."

Mom's eyes bulged as she faced me. "You found that letter?"

"Wait," I said. "Did you know he was going to send one?"

"I hoped he wouldn't," Mom said. "When I didn't see it in the mail, I thought he finally stopped. I can't believe you didn't tell me that you found it. And you lied to me about writing to him! After I told you I didn't want you to." She was yelling now.

I went over her words in my head again. She *knew* that Marcus was going to send me a letter? I couldn't believe it.

"*You're* the reason I never got any of Marcus's other letters?" I asked.

"I told you, I don't want you communicating with him."

"What did you do with them?" I asked. "I want to see them."

"They're gone," Mom said, matter of fact.

"*What?*" I screeched. "Those were my letters."

"Watch your tone, Zoe," Mom said.

I ignored her. "Did you read them? What did they say?" I asked.

Mom shook her head. "I didn't read them."

Anger flashed through me as I imagined a bunch of unopened letters from Marcus sitting in a landfill somewhere, covered in trash. Now I'd never get to read them, and it was all my mom's fault. How could she be so selfish? How could she have lied to me this whole time?

I opened my mouth again, to demand more answers, but before I could say anything else, the doorbell rang.

Chapter Thirty-Two

Mom's face twisted in annoyance as she went to open the door.

"Patricia. Hi," she said. Trevor's mom.

"Hi, Natalie," Patricia said. "I brought Trevor over to apologize for his part in whatever happened today. Also, he wouldn't tell me the whole story, so I hope Zoe will fill in the blanks."

"Come on in," Mom said, and then Patricia and Trevor walked into the living room. He looked at me with worry in his eyes before sitting down on the other side of the couch. I put on my best "I'm sorry" face, hoping he understood. I was the one who'd gotten us into this mess.

"I still don't understand what happened either," Mom said, glaring at Grandma before her gaze landed on me. "Zoe, I'm only going to ask you one time, and you better tell the truth. What were you two doing in a cab?"

"It was my fault," I said. "I made Trevor go to Harvard Square with me."

Mom's face scrunched up even more. "Why?"

"Marcus is innocent!" The words burst out of my mouth, and then without meaning to, I started to cry again. "He's not a murderer. He didn't do it! There's a woman who works at Harvard who says she remembers seeing him when the crime happened." I didn't know for sure yet if that was true—if Professor Thomas really saw Marcus during the crime. All I knew was that she recognized him, but everything inside of me hoped it was true—that he really was innocent.

Out of the corner of my eye, I could see Trevor staring at me, his face twisted in confusion.

I turned to him. "I tried to tell you in the car. Professor Thomas emailed me to say she remembers Marcus."

My mother looked like she didn't know how to begin to respond. "Zoe, I don't know where you got this information, but Marcus is not innocent of murder. He's in prison right now because he's guilty."

"No!" I got up and grabbed my phone from the armchair. I opened my mail app and the email from Professor Thomas. "Here, call her. Her name is Susan Thomas. Marcus's lawyer never looked for her, but I did. I found her, and she remembers him. Call her and she'll tell you what happened."

Mom took the phone from me, and for a moment, I was filled with relief when I thought that she was going to call Professor Thomas back and learn the truth.

But that's not what she did. My phone chimed as she turned it off. "Absolutely not. You are grounded until further notice. No phone and no computer."

"But—"

"And you can forget about auditioning for that Food Network show."

"What?" I asked, my eyes filling with fresh tears. "You can't!"

"I can," Mom said.

Patricia said, "C'mon, Trevor. I need to get ready for work. I'll talk to you about your punishment later. I'm thinking no basketball for a while."

Trevor groaned and didn't look at me before following his mom back into their own house.

Mom made me go to my room, where she took away my computer. Then she went back to the living room with Grandma. I stood next to my door and listened to them argue.

"Natalie," I heard Grandma say when Mom got back to the living room. "I understand why you're mad, but—"

"I don't want to hear anything else," Mom said. "I'm so angry, I can't even look at you. You should just go home."

"Okay," Grandma said. "I hope that once you've calmed down, you see that I was trying to do the right thing."

I imagined Mom rolling her eyes.

"But before I go," Grandma said, "I should also tell you that I let Zoe talk to Marcus on the phone."

No, I thought. *Don't tell her that!*

"You *what?*" Mom screamed, her volume reaching a new decibel. "How could you be so irresponsible?"

"You can't tell me you believe Marcus is guilty of murder. This is *Marcus,* the boy you used to love. I know he broke your heart, but that doesn't mean he doesn't deserve to know his own daughter."

"If you ever, *ever* go behind my back like that again," Mom said slowly, "I will not let you see Zoe anymore. Do you hear me?"

"I hear you," Grandma said. "And I'm sorry."

"Okay," Mom said. "Now, please just go."

When I heard the front door open and close, I shut my bedroom door and sat down on my bed. All I could think about was how Mom would never let me find out what Professor Thomas remembered about Marcus. Or get Marcus's letter back from her.

The truth was right there waiting for me, but it still felt so impossibly far away.

Chapter Thirty-Three

That night, I slept terribly. I dreamed of Marcus sitting alone in his prison cell at the end of a long hallway. I tried to run to him, but every time I got close, the hallway would stretch out even longer and I'd have to start running all over again.

I also dreamed that I was able to call Professor Thomas, but when she told me she remembered Marcus, it was from the news, from when he was convicted of murder. In the dream, Professor Thomas kept laughing at me and saying things like, "Of course he's guilty, silly girl." Lincoln and Sean even showed up out of nowhere and joined in the laughter.

I woke up early the next morning in a cold sweat.

Grandma came by as usual before Mom and Dad left for work. I stayed in my room when she arrived, but from what I could hear, Dad was the only one who said goodbye to her on his way out.

Maya was going to be home that weekend, but it wasn't like I'd get to see her while I was grounded. I wondered how bad Trevor's punishment ended up. If his mom was really going to make him quit basketball, he must've been really sad. I knew how he felt. I'd been so sure that my parents would let me audition for *Kids Bake Challenge!*, since I'd worked so hard at Ari's Cakes all summer. But I could forget about that now. It wasn't fair.

I thought of Professor Thomas waiting for me to write or call back. She probably wondered what was taking me so long. I worried that she'd throw away the letter if I didn't get back to her soon.

I lay in bed most of the day, reading and writing in my journal. I reread all of Marcus's letters that I still had, and wrote him letters that I wasn't sure I'd get to mail anytime soon. Maybe ever. First, I wrote all about finding his alibi witness, and that Professor Thomas actually remembered him. I also wrote about getting in trouble with my parents, and how Mom admitted she'd thrown away his past letters.

In another letter, I wrote about myself. I told him about Hawaiian-ish pizza, asking him if he also liked pepperoni with pineapples. I told him about the only time I'd broken a bone, when I let Trevor convince me that skateboarding down our porch steps was a good idea a few years earlier. I'd broken my left wrist. I wrote about my favorite things to bake, describing all of the recipes in detail.

Except for letting me know that she made me a sandwich for lunch, Grandma left me alone.

On Monday morning, I got ready for the last day of my internship. It was Labor Day, so both of my parents had the day off from work.

"Are you ready to go?" I asked Dad when he was by himself in the kitchen.

"Sorry, kiddo," Dad said. "No internship today, because you're still grounded. We didn't want to inconvenience Ariana, but Mom talked to her yesterday, and she said they'll be fine without your help today."

"What? That's not fair," I mumbled under my breath before going back to my room and putting my pajama pants back on. I wondered if Ariana was selling a special Labor Day cupcake. If the shop was as crowded as it'd been on the Fourth of July. If I'd ever get to share my cereal cupcakes with her.

The next day was my first day of seventh grade.

In the morning, I was in the living room filling my backpack with the new notebooks Mom bought for me over the weekend when Trevor's storm door creaked open and shut. I glanced out the window to find Trevor already walking down the porch steps, wearing a Medford Middle School Basketball T-shirt and jeans.

I threw my lunch bag into my backpack, zipped it up, and slipped on my sneakers. I shouted, "Going to the bus!" so Mom and Dad knew I was leaving. Then I ran outside to catch up with Trevor a couple houses down. "Trevor," I said. "Wait up."

He stopped walking and glanced back at me. "Hey."

"I've been dying to talk to you. How are you?" I nodded toward his shirt. "Did your mom make you quit the team?"

He glanced down at his shirt and shook his head. "No. I mean, the season hasn't started yet. Hopefully Mom will forget by the time it does."

"That's lucky."

"Well, I was supposed to go to a few Celtics games, but now they're giving the tickets to my uncle and cousins," Trevor said.

"I'm sorry. It's totally my fault."

"Nah, it's okay," he said. "I wanted to help you, and it was worth it."

"So you don't hate me for getting you in trouble?" I asked.

"No! I mean, it sucked getting caught, but I'm glad I could help you learn the truth about Marcus. Going to Harvard was pretty fun, too. Definitely the most exciting thing I got to do all summer."

I had to smile. "Same here."

"Did you get your parents to call Professor Thomas?" he asked.

I frowned. "No. And I still don't have my phone or computer back."

"That stinks. But maybe your parents will change their minds," Trevor said.

"Doesn't seem like that's gonna happen. Mom's still so mad."

We got to our bus stop, and a couple minutes later, the bus pulled up and we got on.

"Zooo-eeeee!" Maya grinned and waved her arms at me from our usual spot in the middle of the bus. Her thick brown hair was in a French braid, and she'd gotten new red glasses.

"Maya! Hi!" I sat down next to her, and she slammed me with a hug. I smiled as I hugged her back, my first real smile since I'd been grounded.

"I missed you," she said.

"Missed you too," I said.

She elbowed me. "Why didn't you answer any of my texts this weekend?"

"I couldn't. Mom took my phone away."

"What? Why?"

"Long story," I said. "I have so much to tell you."

"I have sooo much to tell you, *too*."

I glanced up to see where Trevor had gone. He was sitting in an empty seat a couple of rows ahead of us. "Trevor," I called out, and he turned around. I pointed to the empty seat across from mine, and then moved my backpack over to it. "Do you care?" I asked Maya.

"Fine with me," Maya said.

I waved Trevor over and let him into the seat next to me.

"I was gonna play my Mario game but . . . ," Trevor began.

"No phone?" I finished, and Trevor nodded. "That's okay. You can hang out with us."

He smiled.

The next bus stop would've been where Jasmine and her twin brother got on. But they were all the way in Maryland.

"Have you heard from Jasmine?" I asked Maya.

"Yeah, she sent us a text last night," Maya said. "She says she misses us and she starts at her new school today."

School wouldn't be the same without Jasmine, but I was so happy to be here with Maya and Trevor. I couldn't wait to tell Maya all about Marcus and the Harvard adventure, but that could wait until lunch, when we had more time.

"Oh! I have something for you," Maya said, reaching into her backpack. She pulled out a package of assorted Ghirardelli chocolate and passed it to me. "I got it from their shop in San Francisco."

"Thanks!" I said, opening the package. It was never too early for chocolate. But before I took one for myself, I held the package out to Trevor, who had been watching me carefully. "I know you want some."

His eyes lit up as he took a few pieces for himself, immediately opening one and stuffing it into his mouth.

I ate a piece of chocolate too. It was nice to be surrounded by my friends again.

But then I thought about Marcus, sitting alone in his prison cell, and my stomach churned.

"You know what, you can have these," I told Trevor and handed him the rest of the chocolates.

Chapter Thirty-Four

"Hey, Zo," Dad said as he poked his head into my room a couple of days later, while I was doing French homework.

The clock on my wall said it was only four o'clock. "What are you doing home so early?" I asked.

"We have something to talk to you about."

"We?"

Dad opened the door wider and he, Mom, and Grandma walked into my room. What was Mom doing home early, too? They all stood in a line in front of me, and I braced myself for yelling, or more punishment, or something else equally terrible. Then I noticed Mom seemed upset—her eyes were slightly red, and her mascara was smeared. Had she been crying?

"What's going on?" I asked, scanning their faces.

Mom cleared her throat before saying, "I spoke to Professor Thomas today."

I sat up straighter. "You did? What? How?"

She nodded. "Your grandma convinced me that it was the right thing to do."

I looked over at Grandma, who smiled at me.

"Oh my goodness," I said, grinning back at her, my head spinning. I couldn't believe what I was hearing. "Thank you!"

"Professor Thomas told me what happened when you went to her office. She said that she had your letter from Marcus." Mom reached into her blazer pocket and held out a folded piece of loose-leaf paper. "Here."

Marcus's letter.

"You went to *see* Professor Thomas?"

Mom nodded. "After our phone call."

"We both went so we could talk to her together," Dad said.

I couldn't believe it. "Does she really remember Marcus?" I asked.

"Yes," Mom said. "She had a lot to say."

Dad said, "I asked her if I could record our conversation. We want to talk to a lawyer about what she said."

A lawyer? My heart squeezed. They were going to talk to a lawyer about this?

Dad took his cell phone out, and a moment later, Professor Thomas's voice filled my bedroom. My heart started to race as I leaned closer to the phone in Dad's hand.

"Let me start from the beginning," Professor Thomas said. "Marcus originally reached out to me because he wanted to see a futon I was selling—I'd posted it on Craigslist. He came by my house to take a look."

Dad's voice came up on the recording. "You're sure it was that same day? His crime took place on October 26. It sounds like police believe the victim was killed in the late afternoon."

"Yes, I'm pretty sure. It was a Friday," Professor Thomas said. "He came toward the end of the workday. I showed him the futon, and he said he wanted to buy it. Then he noticed some of the baby stuff I had out for sale, which my brother and his wife were getting rid of. Marcus said he was going to be a dad soon, and started asking me questions about the baby stuff. Like what sort of gear he should have."

"He said he wanted to buy stuff for a baby?" Mom's voice on the recording asked. She sounded surprised, but in a good way.

"Yes," Professor Thomas said. "That's the part that made me remember him. He said he could use some stuff for his 'Little Tomato,' which is what he said he called the baby. I thought that was so cute. He was so young, still looked like a kid himself, but he seemed excited to become a dad. I'd never heard of Little Tomato before. My brother called his son Peanut at one point. I asked him where he got the nickname, and he said it was from a song. He ended up turning on his car and playing it for me. It was a sweet song."

The tune of "Hang On Little Tomato" played in my head as I listened to Professor Thomas tell the story. I could imagine it—them standing in her driveway listening to the song from his car's speakers. Marcus smiling, thinking of me.

Because he wasn't committing a crime that afternoon. He was thinking about me. My eyes started to water.

Professor Thomas kept talking. "We talked about babies for a couple of minutes, and then we decided on a price for the futon. He said he'd rent a U-Haul truck the next morning so he could bring it home, but that he'd give me the cash that night so I'd hold the futon for him.

He asked me where the nearest ATM was, and I said there was one a few blocks away in downtown Brookline. I remember he ended up walking there. He left his car in front of my house.

"He didn't come back right away, and I remember wondering if he'd gotten lost. But then he came back holding a coffee cup and a bag of doughnuts. By that point, it was getting dark out. My husband got home, and he and Marcus got into a conversation about sports, because my husband had a Boston Celtics hat on, and I guess Marcus is a big fan. They talked for a while. But then Marcus said he didn't need the futon after all. I guess while he was gone, he got a call from a friend who said he could have his couch. Marcus left sometime after that."

Dad stopped the recording there.

I blinked at them. "Do you believe her?" I asked, looking between Mom, Dad, and Grandma. "Do you think she really did see Marcus that afternoon?"

Grandma nodded, and Dad said, "Her story makes sense. Plus, it takes at least thirty minutes to drive back and forth between UMass Boston and Brookline, where Professor Thomas lived. I'm not an expert, but I don't see how Marcus could've driven back and forth, spent all that time in Brookline, and still committed the crime near campus."

"What do you think?" I asked Mom.

She sighed. "I don't know what to think. I'm still in shock. I spent so long convincing myself he had to be guilty. It was easier to believe that, to justify him being in prison—away from us." She teared up again, blinking them away, and cleared her throat. "But he could be innocent, and if he is, I need to know. We have to find out the truth."

I could barely believe my ears. "What happens now?"

"After we left Harvard, I called a friend of mine who's a lawyer," Dad said. "He's not a criminal lawyer, but he has friends from law school who are. He's going to speak to a couple of them and see what we can do. He said the Innocence Project of New England is right here in Boston, so we can reach out to them."

"I know about them!" I said. "Do you think Marcus will be able to get out of prison?"

"We don't know," Grandma said. "Finding his alibi witness was only the first step. That's why we need to find him a *good* lawyer."

We. They were really going to help! "I . . . I still can't believe you talked to Professor Thomas," I said.

"You did a good job with your investigating," Dad said, his voice now turning serious. "But that doesn't excuse your lying and going to Harvard without permission. That was really dangerous."

"So I'm still grounded?"

"Yes," Mom said.

I nodded, not even a little bit upset. How could I care about being grounded after finding out that Marcus's alibi was true? And he might get out of prison?

I stood up, and by the time I took a couple steps to Mom, my eyes were watering for real. "Thank you," I told her. Then I took one more step closer and tightly wrapped my arms around her middle.

Mom didn't say anything, but squeezed me back and swayed with me for a couple seconds. Her hug felt so familiar and comforting. I'd missed this. I'd missed her so much. I cried into her blouse.

When we separated, Mom wiped the tears from both my eyes and hers. "If you want to talk some more about Marcus," she said, "you can let me know. I understand that he's part of your life now."

"Really?" I asked. I couldn't believe my luck.

"Really."

"My turn," Grandma said, and she pulled me into a hug.

"I didn't mean what I said," I told her. "I don't hate you. You know that, right?"

"Of course I know that, baby girl," Grandma said. "You were angry. Don't worry about it. I'm still proud of you," she whispered into my ear.

I grinned, feeling proud of me, too.

That night, I couldn't help it. I wrote an actual letter to Marcus on my stationery. I didn't know when I'd get to mail it, but I hoped it would be soon.

From the Desk of Zoe Washington

September 8

Dear Marcus,

You won't believe this. I found Susan Thomas! I've been calling her Professor Thomas because she teaches at Harvard. What's even better is that she remembers you from the afternoon of the crime. Dad's lawyer friends are going to reach out to the Innocence Project, to see if they will help. I'm really excited and hope this means you'll get out of prison.

No matter what happens, I want you to know that I'm really glad I'm getting to know you.

Love,

Zoe

PS Send another song for my playlist, okay?

Chapter Thirty-Five

On Saturday, I went to the kitchen to get breakfast and was surprised to see a few of my baking supplies set up on the island. An apron was folded neatly beside them, next to my Ruby Willow cookbook. Dad sat on one stool with a steaming mug of coffee in front of him as he flipped through an article on his tablet. Mom sat next to him with a cup of tea and a magazine. They both looked up when I walked in. I was suddenly worried that they'd decided to totally remove all of my baking supplies from the house as part of my grounding. I glanced at my yellow mixer, wondering if I should lunge for it before it was too late.

"Good morning," both my parents said at the same time. Neither of them *sounded* angry, but that didn't mean they weren't.

"What's all this?" I asked, pointing to all my baking stuff.

"We want to bake something," Mom said. "As a family."

"But I thought you said I couldn't bake while I'm grounded."

"We're going to make this one exception. And today you get *two* sous-chefs," Mom said. "Pick a recipe in here, and Dad will run to the store if we're missing anything. Then we'll start after you eat breakfast."

Smiling, I grabbed the cookbook and started skimming through it, but then I realized that what I really wanted to bake wasn't within its pages.

I got a small notepad and pen from our junk drawer. I wrote down the ingredients we needed and handed it to Dad.

"Froot Loops?" he asked, his bushy eyebrows furrowing.

I smiled. "Yup."

"Okay," he said, sounding skeptical. "I'll be right back."

While he was gone, I ate a bowl of oatmeal with sliced bananas. "You know, I made this playlist with songs

Marcus sent me in his letters," I told Mom. "Plus some others by the same artists. I called it my 'Little Tomato' playlist."

"That's sweet," she said. "Can I hear it?"

I grabbed my phone and hooked it up to the speakers, and Jill Scott's "Golden" came on.

Mom immediately started singing along—sounding even better than when she sang to herself in front of the bathroom mirror.

We danced around the kitchen and sang along with the songs on the playlist while we waited for Dad to come back from the store. By the time he walked into the kitchen with a grocery bag, we were belting along to Boyz II Men and Mariah Carey's "One Sweet Day," and he looked at us like we were the silliest people in the world.

I lowered the music and grabbed the cereal box from the grocery bag. The first thing I did was pour some of the cereal into a bowl with milk to soak.

"I came up with a cupcake recipe," I explained.

"With cereal?" Mom asked.

"Yes. Wait until you try them."

When the cereal milk was ready, we got to work making the cupcakes. Mom and Dad helped with each of the steps—creaming the butter and sugar together, adding the flour and cereal milk and other ingredients. When the batter was done, I separated it into three bowls and we added the red, blue, and green food coloring. I used an ice cream scoop to drop small amounts of each color batter into each cupcake tin, and then we used toothpicks to swirl the batter around a little.

While the cupcakes baked, we worked on a butter-cream frosting and danced some more to the Little Tomato playlist. When the song "Hang On Little Tomato" came on, Dad stopped what he was doing and paid closer attention to it.

"Oh, I like the sound of this one," he said.

"I knew you would," I told him.

When the cupcakes were all done and the whole room smelled like sugar, we set them out to cool on the kitchen island. The tie-dye colors came out perfect. We put the white buttercream frosting into a plastic bag and cut the tip. I showed them how to frost the cupcakes, and we each did a few. When they were done, they didn't look as perfect as Liz's cupcakes at Ari's Cakes, but they still looked pretty professional.

"Last step," I said, grabbing the Froot Loops box. I scooped some of the cereal out and sprinkled a few pieces on top of each cupcake.

"Ta da!" I said.

"They look so pretty," Mom said. She picked one up and put it on a white plate, then moved it to a sunny spot on the counter. She grabbed her phone to snap a picture. "Seriously, look how pretty this looks. I'm sending this to Ari."

I swelled with pride.

"But how do they *taste*?" Dad asked.

We each grabbed a cupcake. As soon as I finished my first bite, I knew I'd nailed the recipe. It tasted just like the Froot Loops, but not too sweet, and the buttercream frosting was creamy and delicious.

"You know, I wasn't sure about cereal in cupcakes, but you really know what you're doing," Dad said. "This is amazing."

Mom still had cupcake in her mouth, so she nodded and smiled.

I beamed.

Dad's cell phone rang, and he stared at the screen. "It's Jason. I should take this." Jason was Dad's lawyer friend who was able to get us a meeting with the Innocence Project for the following week. I didn't know what would come of it, but I thought about the stories from *The Wrongfully Convicted* book and tried to stay hopeful.

While Dad was gone, Mom and I started to clean up.

"Can I ask you something? Well, two somethings?" I

licked icing off a spoon and put it in the dishwasher.

"Of course," Mom said.

"Do you think you can forgive Marcus now?"

"Oh, honey," she said, putting her hand on my shoulder. "If Marcus really is innocent, I hope you will forgive me for keeping him from you all these years. I hope you understand why I did it, that I was only trying to protect you. I still am, the best way I know how."

I leaned over and wrapped my arms around Mom's waist, and we gave each other a big squeeze. "It's okay. I forgive you."

Mom exhaled and then twisted around to grab a paper towel from the kitchen counter. After dabbing her eyes with it, she said, "I don't know what's going to happen with Marcus, with these lawyers, but your dad, Grandma, and I are here for you no matter what, okay? We love you."

"I love you, too," I said, and Mom kissed my forehead.

"What was the other something you wanted to ask?"

"Oh. One second." I ran to my room to grab my letter to Marcus. When I got back to the kitchen, I showed her the envelope.

She stared at it for a second, and I tried to read her face.

"I was hoping you'd let me mail it," I said. "You can read it first, if you want."

She didn't take the envelope from me, to read it or rip it into pieces. Instead, she went into the junk drawer and grabbed a stamp. "Why don't we go mail it right now? I can walk to the mailbox with you."

My eyes lit up. "Okay."

Mom put Butternut on a leash and we all headed outside. We walked down the street toward the mailbox, Mom's arm linked through mine the whole way.

Chapter Thirty-Six

It was a little scary to visit a prison. First, we went through security, and then a uniformed guard led us down an empty hallway to the visiting room. Our shoes tapped against the linoleum floor, and the fluorescent lights above us were so bright. It felt like we were being led to our own prison cells. I grabbed Mom's hand. On the other side of her were Dad and Grandma. I breathed in and out. They would keep me safe.

The visiting room was pretty plain. It had tables and chairs and a couple of vending machines in the corner. A few visitors were already at tables, sitting across from inmates—men in orange jumpsuits. One woman clutched an inmate's hands from across the table and laughed with him about something. He looked really happy to see her, too.

In a few minutes, that would be me, seeing Marcus in person for the first time ever. I couldn't smile yet, though. I was too shaky with nerves.

We found seats at an empty table, and Grandma took a few coins out of her bag. "I know you're sad you couldn't bring your cupcakes today, but why don't you get Marcus something from the vending machine?"

I *was* still bummed that I couldn't bring the cupcakes. I really wanted Marcus to be able to taste some of my baking. But hopefully he'd get to try my desserts soon, outside of prison. The Innocence Project lawyers were working with him on that. Dad told me they were feeling optimistic.

At least I could show Marcus pictures I'd printed out of them in the window display at Ari's Cakes. Mom had given Ariana one of my cereal cupcakes to try, and she loved them so much, she made it the special flavor for the month of October. She even put my name on the sign as the featured baker. I didn't care anymore that I didn't get to audition for *Kids Bake Challenge!* How many kids got to say their cupcake recipe was for sale in a real bakery? Not even Ruby Willow had done that. Forget about becoming a pastry chef when I grew up. I already *was* one.

I took the change from Grandma and went to the

vending machine. I stared at the snack options and wondered what kind Marcus liked best. Peanut butter cups? Sour cream and onion chips? Did he like sweet or savory? Or maybe he was like me, and liked them both at the same time. I finally decided on peanut M&M's. I put the quarters in and the bag plopped out at the bottom of the machine.

When I turned back around, I stopped breathing and almost dropped the candy. Marcus had come into the room, and he was standing in front of our table, looking right at me. I recognized him right away. His face was the same as in my photo of him, except older, of course, and his cheeks were fuller. He looked freshly shaven. Even wearing his prison clothes, he was handsome.

Marcus smiled really big, and it lit up his whole face. Soon his eyes filled up with tears. He motioned me over, and somehow my legs carried me toward him. He was tall—a couple of inches taller than Dad.

"My Little Tomato. My Zoe," he said as he stood in front of me and took me in. "I can't believe you're here. Finally."

As soon as I heard him say "Little Tomato," I relaxed. He sounded just like on the phone, except he was here—in real life. I couldn't believe it. I smiled back, and I knew we must look like twins, since our smiles were so similar. I wished I could take a picture, but phones weren't allowed in the room.

There was something I could do. I put the candy on the table and moved closer to give Marcus a hug. He squeezed me tight, and I could smell the detergent on his clothing. Tears started to fall from my own eyes.

After our hug, we all sat down around the table.

Grandma reached over and squeezed Marcus's hand. "It's really nice to see you."

"You too," Marcus said, and then he looked at Mom. "Natalie, thanks for coming. For bringing Zoe."

"It's about time she got to see you." Mom teared up. "I'm sorry it took this long."

"It's okay. I understand." Marcus looked at Dad and said, "Paul. Thank you for stepping in and being such a great father to Zoe when I couldn't. I'm so grateful."

Dad shook his head. "I'm the one who's grateful. Zoe's an amazing kid."

"Well, I'm thirsty," Grandma said, standing up. "Anyone else? Natalie, Paul, want to come to the vending machines with me?"

I knew what Grandma was doing—giving me some alone time with Marcus. Mom squeezed my shoulder before she and Dad walked away from our table.

Marcus smiled at me again. "How are things? Tell me what's going on with you."

"I'm great, especially now that I'm here," I said.

"Seventh grade is good so far. And look, I brought a picture of my cupcake on display at Ari's Cakes."

I handed the photo to him and he smiled at it. "Look at that. Wish I could try them."

"You will," I said.

"What else's going on?"

"I've been hanging out with my friends Trevor and Maya." I told him how the three of us started doing more stuff together, and sometimes Trevor's basketball teammates—not Lincoln or Sean—joined us. Trevor stopped hanging out with Lincoln and Sean, but there were other, nicer guys on the team. Maya and I started going to the basketball games to cheer from the bleachers. I'd bake brownies or other treats for us to snack on during the games.

"I'm so happy that you're happy," he said. "I can't wait to see what your life is like for myself one day."

"I can't wait either," I said.

"When I'm out, we can go to a Celtics game together," Marcus said. "Have you ever been to one?"

"No, but I'd like to," I said. "Can Trevor come, too? He loves the Celtics."

"Smart guy. Of course he can come. Can't wait to meet him."

"I told Trevor all about how you play basketball. We

can all play together in our driveway. I've been beating him at horse lately."

"That's my girl," he said, laughing.

My eyes landed on the peanut M&M's on the table, and I remembered what I'd been wondering earlier. "Hey, do you like sweet or savory foods better?"

"You know, I like a mix of both. I used to always like eating candy and chips at the same time."

"Me too!" I said.

We spent the next hour talking about other things we had in common—he liked Hawaiian-ish pizza too! After a while, I was able to forget we were in a prison visiting room.

Eventually visiting hours ended, and we had to say our goodbyes. We gave each other a long hug and I tried not to cry, so Marcus wouldn't. I knew there'd be more letters and phone calls between us, but what I really wanted was to do this more. To be able to see him in person whenever I wanted, and not within these prison walls.

I had no idea what would happen next, but I hoped with all my heart that the Innocence Project would set Marcus free. In the meantime, I was so thankful that I'd found his letter on my twelfth birthday, and that he was in my life now, where he belonged.

Epilogue

"Happy birthday to Marcus," everyone sang. "Happy birthday to you!"

Marcus leaned over the Celtics-themed cake, silently made a wish, and blew out the candles. Everyone cheered, and I looked around at all the smiling faces. Mom, Dad, and Grandma. Trevor and his parents. Maya. Ariana and her husband.

Marcus was actually there, in my house, celebrating his birthday. I still couldn't believe it. The process of appealing his guilty verdict took a lot longer than I expected—years instead of months. But once his lawyers at the Innocence Project finally got him a new trial, they made a strong case to prove his innocence. They explored new DNA evidence and named a new suspect—another man who had lived in Lucy's building. In the end, Marcus's conviction was overturned, and that other man ended up being found guilty of the crime. I cried so hard when I heard the judge name Marcus "not guilty." We all did.

Not only did Marcus get justice, but Lucy's family did, too.

Now, Marcus wore jeans and a green Celtics T-shirt, which was one of the gifts I gave him after he came out of prison. In it, he really looked like an older version of the Marcus from my first picture of him.

His parents—my grandparents—were also there. They'd flown up from Atlanta for the party. I first got to meet them during Marcus's new trial, so it was nice to see them again.

"Let's cut the cake!" Trevor said. "It is chocolate, right?"

"Sorry, Trevor," I said.

"Aw, man," he said.

Dad started cutting the cake and Mom helped him with the plates. Marcus took the first slice, and I took the second one, even though I was still full from all the food. I'd helped Marcus make macaroni and cheese, and he also made barbecued ribs that turned out really yummy.

His mom helped my parents make a bunch of food, too. He was right—she was an amazing cook.

Still, there was always room for dessert. Especially when it was the cake I helped make at Ari's Cakes. It was a two-tiered cake made with my cereal cupcake recipe. I'd done some more experimenting with cake flavors since then, but this recipe felt right for today, since it reminded me of the summer I first started writing to Marcus.

Marcus came up next to me. "Hey, Zoe, I want to give you your present now."

"What? It's your birthday!" I said. "And I still haven't given you my gift." I'd gotten him some cooking supplies—an apron embroidered with "Big Tomato," my nickname for him, and a nice cast iron pan.

"I know, but there's something I really wanted to get you," Marcus said. "Come to the living room with me."

I knew Marcus didn't have a lot of money yet. He was working two part-time jobs—one in the office of a legal nonprofit organization in Boston, and he also started assisting Vincent at Ari's Cakes. After hearing about his cooking experience while in prison, Ariana took a chance on Marcus and gave him a job. It was Mom who'd suggested it, since she knew Ariana was looking to hire more staff.

Grandma said Marcus was lucky. A lot of men who got out of prison—whether they were truly guilty or not—had trouble finding jobs. Marcus was saving up to be able to rent his own apartment. He was staying in Grandma's guest room in the meantime.

I'd get to work alongside Marcus at the bakery the next summer—this time, as a real employee, since I'd finally be old enough. I never got to audition for *Kids Bake Challenge!* The Food Network ended up canceling the show. But I was still going to be a professional baker with several cookbooks one day. It would happen no matter what.

In the living room, there was a large rectangular box covered in purple wrapping paper on the coffee table. We both sat down on the couch, but Marcus couldn't sit still, clearly excited for me to see whatever was inside. "Go ahead, open it," he said.

I started ripping the wrapping paper off.

"You got me a record player?" I said. "This is so cool."

Marcus grinned at me. "Let's plug it in."

"I don't have any records," I said.

"I thought of that." He pulled a gift bag from behind the couch. "I got you a few to start you off."

"Oh my gosh!" I flipped through the records, and they were artists from my Little Tomato playlist: Lauryn Hill, Boyz II Men, and Stevie Wonder. "Thank you! How did you get all of these?"

"I worked some extra shifts at the bakery," Marcus said. "There's one song I really want to play for you." He unwrapped the Stevie Wonder album, which was called *Hotter Than July*. He got up, found a plug for the record player, and turned it on.

"The one thing about records," Marcus said, "is that you can't skip songs too easily. The one I want you to hear is the last track, so I have to guess where to put the needle."

I watched as he carefully positioned the record on the turntable and gently placed the needle on it. The record started spinning and Stevie Wonder's voice filled the room.

Marcus smiled. "Now, doesn't he sound especially good?"

"Yeah," I said. "He has such a great voice."

The current song ended and a new one started.

"Okay, this is the one I wanted you to hear," Marcus said. "Dance with me."

"Right here?" I asked.

"Yeah, right here. C'mon." Marcus grabbed my hands and we started dancing to the upbeat music.

And then the chorus started. "*Happy birthday to ya. Happy birthday to ya. Happy birthday!*" Stevie sang.

"Oh!" I said.

"This is the best version of the happy birthday song, hands down," Marcus said. "It's got flavor." He spun me around and around, and I laughed.

When the chorus came on again, we sang along.

Then Grandma walked into the room, followed by Mom and Dad.

"What's going on in here?" Mom asked.

"We're dancing. Join us!" I said.

They did, and together, we danced and sang along with the song. Mom belted out some harmonies.

It was hard to believe that Marcus was once a total stranger to me. And now, he was here and we were having a dance party. He was out of prison because of me.

When the song ended, Marcus and I both collapsed on the couch with big, identical smiles, and I felt grateful and happy and full.

Acknowledgments

My journey from aspiring writer to published author was long, a lot longer than I expected. I couldn't have gotten to this point without my sheer determination, countless cups of coffee, or all the following people who supported me along the way.

Thank you to my agent, Alex Slater, for championing Zoe's story from the very beginning. Deciding to work with you was the easiest and best decision I've made! You helped me get my dream book deal, and I will be forever grateful. I also want to thank Nicola DeRobertis-Theye for bringing Zoe overseas, and the rest of the Trident Media Group team for their passion and hard work.

To Alexandra Arnold, who acquired this book before leaving her role at Katherine Tegen Books, I'm so glad I was able to work with you to strengthen this manuscript. You are incredible at what you do! You told me I would be in good hands with my new editor, Mabel Hsu, and you were right. Mabel, you've been amazing to work with. Thank you for always treating my debut as if it was your own acquisition. To the rest of the team at Katherine Tegen Books—Tanu Srivastava, Liz Byer, Mark Rifkin, Erin Wallace, Kristen Eckhardt, Vaishali Nayak, Laura Mock, Amy Ryan, Sam Benson, and Megan Gendell—thank you for all your hard work. Thank you as well to Mirelle Ortega for illustrating my beautiful cover.

One of the rewarding parts of having a long publishing journey is all the writer friends I made throughout the years. Thank you to my New School MFA crew—Kathryn Holmes, Michael Dobbs, Elizabeth Dunn-Ruiz, Benjamin Andrew Moore, Gabriela Pereira, and Mia Garcia—who've been there since I was a newbie writing my very first novel. You all continue to inspire me, and I'm so grateful for our friendship. To my CT Novelists—Jessica Bayliss, Cristina Dos Santos, Ginger Merante, and Juliana Haygert—you four are my rocks! I also want to thank the other writers who've encouraged me over the years: Dahlia Adler, Ellen Goodlett, and Emery Lord. To all my other writer friends who I met online or at conferences: thank you for your support! I also want to thank my friends who aren't writers but who've always been excited to hear updates about my work, which meant the world to me: Jenifer Parker, Laura Wolther, Maura FitzGerald, and Shaderi Taylor (RIP).

To my critique group ladies—Jodi Kendall, Gina Carey, and Alexandra Alger—I can always count on you for insightful feedback and support. Thank you for helping me bring Zoe's story to light. A special thank-you to the other authors who took time to read this book and provide feedback. Kacen Callender, thank you for helping me realize that this was, in fact, meant to be a middle grade book, and not YA. Karen Strong, you've been Zoe's cheerleader from the start, and a wonderful friend. I can't wait for us to do an event together. Dana Alison Levy, your thorough notes and mentorship while I was revising were priceless.

To the Shoreline Arts Alliance Tassy Walden Committee: thank you for selecting this story for the 2017 middle grade award. It was an incredible honor and the best kind of validation as I prepared to query literary agents.

I'm so happy to be a member of the Roaring 20s debut group—and not only because of the awesome name. The camaraderie and support of the group has been incredible. A special shout-out to Lorien Lawrence, Tanya Guerrero, and Shannon Doleski for all our chats leading up to our debut year. I'm also grateful for my fellow Class of 2K20 Books members.

I've loved reading and writing my entire life, but I wouldn't have tried to get a book published if it wasn't for my mother, my biggest supporter. Mom, thank you for always encouraging me to chase my dreams, no matter how farfetched they seemed. (Let's be honest, I was never going to make it to Broadway! But you drove me to all those acting classes, dance classes, and singing lessons anyway.) When I switched gears to creative writing, your continued belief in me carried me through my decade-long journey to publication.

To Dad, thank you for always being so supportive and for answering all my legal questions!

To Steve, the love of my life. You are the best husband I could've asked for. Thank you for being there for all the highs and lows of getting this book published and for always believing in me.

To Luna: I started writing this book when you were only a few months old. I'm so happy that you're able to see me accomplish this dream, so you know that you can absolutely do the same. Shine bright, baby girl.

To all the young writers and aspiring authors reading

this, longing for the day when you'll get to write your own acknowledgments for your own debut book: keep writing. This book is proof that hard work pays off and dreams do come true. I'm rooting for you.

Finally, thank you to all my readers. I'm thrilled that I was able to share Zoe's story with you, and I truly hope you enjoyed it.